A HEART REDEEMED

A HEART REDEEMED

HEART'S INTENT
BOOK SEVEN

DAWN BROWER

CONTENTS

For my Family, without you, I'd probably have run out of ideas a long time ago. I might become...crabby from time to time, but I love you. I'm blessed to have you in my life, especially on the darkest of days when their doesn't seem any hope to find any light. Thank you for supporting me. There are not words to tell you how much I appreciate everything you do for me.

PROLOGUE

The sun had set in the sky, leaving an orange glow that outlined the house. Enzo liked it. That ominous delineation almost gave him permission for what he was about to do. He craved it...the authorization to give into his darkest fantasies. Why not acknowledge the deepest truth he held inside of him? His thirst for destruction had always been there, and while he'd given in to it in the past, this time it was personal. His brother had to die, and if his wife and daughter were casualties of that vendetta, so be it. Perhaps he'd make Antony watch as he tortured his wife, then start in on the little girl. Children were always special. Their innocence being wiped from the world at his hands gave him a sense of purpose.

Many would think him wrong, a sociopath, and perhaps they were right, but he didn't care. Why would he? This was his path, and what he'd been born to do. They had tried to beat it out of him as a child, but it only fueled the fire inside him. There was no sunlight inside his soul. He didn't feel anything. The darkness had shrouded him completely and shown him that light was never the answer. It only brought pain. This way he gave pain instead.

He'd wait until the moon's beams were the only light visible. Blackness was his constant companion and would ensure his success. While the glow of orange thrilled him, it would only serve to hamper his mission. He'd hold on to the feeling it gave him until the end.

Soon, he'd be inside the house, and his brother would finally lose everything. Antony would know what it was like to be the one shoved to the ground with a boot to the face. He'd feel pain, and then he'd be no more. Their father would grieve for the good son, the favorite, the one he'd groomed to be the center of attention...a success in the opposite way as the unwanted child—Enzo.

He'd been thrown into an orphanage when his mother had died giving birth. The way he'd been raised... He shuddered. There had been no amenities available to him. It was either die or survive by any means necessary. He chose the latter, and he'd gained a skillset along the way that would rival even the best assassins. He'd even taken on a few select clients and built up a nice egg. One day, maybe when the thrill stopped, he'd retire on his own remote island. He hated people and didn't see any reason to socialize.

His job wasn't done yet though.

He'd been hired to kill his brother. The client didn't realize what he'd hired Enzo to do. Not that it mattered. Antony didn't even know Enzo existed. Their father hadn't bothered to find out if Enzo had lived or died. Enzo had known though. He'd been told many times as a child that his father was a great man. As soon as he was able to comprehend the significance, it had been drilled into him, as if he should bow down and be grateful for being sired by the bastard.

The sun had gone down. It was time. He slid his KA-BAR out of its sheathe and checked the sharpness on a nearby leaf. It slid through the foliage with ease. It would shred soft flesh to nothing. His heart raced inside his chest as anticipation rolled through him. *Soon...* Today his brother would die, and Enzo would finally experience true justice. His father would grieve, and that alone was enough to keep Enzo warm through the rest of his days. He would inflict pain on him, and one day, he'd inform him who had taken his precious son away. Too bad he was infirm and lived in a nursing facility. The pain wouldn't be nearly enough, but it would have to do. In one blow, he'd lose everything—a son, a daughter-in-law, and a granddaughter, and all possibility of carrying on the family line he cherished, for Enzo would never have children. Even if his father was willing to acknowledge him.

MILA GALLO SHOULD BE in bed. Her parents had read her a story and tucked her in over an hour ago. They were in their room, probably sleeping, but she didn't stop to check. She wanted a cookie, maybe three, along with a glass of milk. Before bed, she'd begged for some of them. Earlier that day, she had baked them with her mother, and they were super yummy. She'd been denied her treat, so she had stayed awake, waiting, until she deemed it safe enough to sneak down to the kitchen.

She tiptoed down the stairs and went to the

kitchen, trying to be as silent as possible. Mila wanted those cookies, and if her parents awakened, she'd be denied once again. Her mother had stored them in a cookie jar on the counter. She opened a cupboard door and used a shelf to climb up there. She pulled the jar over and lifted the lid, then slid her hand inside to retrieve two cookies. That would be enough for now. She set them on the counter, then put the lid back on the jar. Once it was back where it had been originally she slid back to the floor.

Footsteps on the stairs caught her attention. Mila gasped, grabbed her cookies, and slid into the other side of the cupboard, the side that her mother usually stored her mixer, but it was still on the counter. She closed the door and huddled inside with her cookies, waiting.

Silently, she prayed she wouldn't be discovered. She was afraid to take a bite of her cookies for fear the crunching would give her location away. Why had she sneaked down for them? Was a cookie really worth being punished by her parents? They might not let her have any more of them after this…

"Why are you doing this?" her father asked. His voice shook a little as he spoke. Who was he talking to? Did she dare peek out? No, she'd wait, patience was the key to staying out of trouble.

"I could enlighten you," a man replied nonchalantly. Mila didn't recognize the voice. She tried to listen harder somehow, but it didn't help. "However I honestly don't care to. There will be no villainous confessions. It's best we get down to business so I can be on my way."

"My wife…" her father choked out the words.

"Is dead," he said with no emotion. "As you too will be soon. Now where is your daughter. She wasn't in her bed."

Mila covered her mouth with her hands to hold in the scream she desperately wanted to release. She started to say the alphabet in her head. Maybe she should silently sing…anything so she didn't give her location away. She closed her eyes tight to try to erase the thought of her mother being gone. What could she do to help her father? If she gave her hiding space away, the bad man might hurt her too. She shook and fought tears. Her mama was dead and she'd never see her again. Pain spread through her in waves. She understood death was final, but had never really experienced what it meant other than in movies. Now…she wanted to forget. None of this seemed real.

"She's not here," her father said. "You can't hurt her."

Her father lied, but she wouldn't hold that against him. He probably had no idea where she'd gone. Her parents loved her, and she had no doubt that they'd die to protect her. A tear slipped down her cheek. She couldn't stop it, but she bit on her lip to hold back the sobs.

"That's a shame," the man said. "I had hoped to torture her in front of you too." What did that mean? Did he hurt her mama a lot before he killed her? He wanted to hurt her like he did her mother. Mila nibbled on her bottom lip. She prayed the bad man wouldn't find her.

"I don't understand any of this." The terror in her father's tone nearly undid her. She squeezed her eyes closed even tighter in an attempt to block it all out. Quiet. She had to be quiet. Had they ever been in their bedroom? She hadn't checked… Where was her mother?

"As much as I would love to carry this on," the evil man said. "I've dallied long enough. Since your daughter is not here, then we might as well dispense with the pretense. It's time for you to die."

"Nooo," her father grunted, and then something hit the floor with a loud *thud*. Was it her father? Had the bad man killed him? She couldn't check. If she got out of the cupboard then he'd find her to, and she didn't want to die. She rocked back and forth in the cupboard, staying silent the entire time. Mila prayed the bad man left, but she had no way of knowing when he did, or if it would ever be safe again…

The cookies she pilfered slid down to the cupboard floor, they were no longer a temptation she could not ignore. They were a reminder of something she'd lost dearly, and after this night, never be able to enjoy.

CHAPTER ONE

The next morning...

Detective Alexander Foster stared at the gruesome sight and frowned. He would never get used to seeing dead bodies, but this, it was nothing like he'd ever witnessed in his entire career on the force. The woman, Cara Gallo had been tortured. Her entire body was covered in slashes, and the blood...it was stomach churning. Lex didn't understand what had happened or why, but the man, Antony Gallo had been killed in the hallway leading to the kitchen by a single knife wound. Why hadn't he fought his attacker? The man had a few abrasions on his face, and some scratches on his forearm, but no real defensive wounds.

It didn't make any kind of sense…

He'd figure it out. It was what he did, and he'd see the person who had harmed these people brought to justice. Lex burned with rage at the tragedy. Two people at the start of their lives together…and now they were dead. He picked up a family photo from a nearby shelf and stared at it. They looked so happy in the picture, and the little girl's smile couldn't get bigger. She had dark hair and eyes the color of the ocean on a sunny day. Her dimples made her appear even more darling.

From her coloring alone, she could be Lex's daughter, though perhaps his own hair was a shade lighter than hers. If she'd been his daughter, he'd have done whatever necessary to protect her. Was that what Antony Gallo had been doing? Had he decided to not fight back to keep her safe somehow? Did the person that killed them take her with them? From the little evidence they had gathered, she was adored by her parents, so it made sense that her father would die to protect her. Where was she though? They had to figure it out and soon.

"The daughter is still missing," his partner, Craig Wilson, said as he came to stand beside him "The deceased male's business partner is over there." He pointed to where a man with dark auburn hair wearing a charcoal suit and sapphire tie stood talking with a patrol officer.

Lex swallowed hard. "He doesn't know where the little girl is?"

"Negative," Craig answered, then brushed his hand through his sandy brown hair in frustration. "He is the one that found the bodies. He came over when Mr. Gallo didn't show up for work. We need to find that little girl."

"We will," Lex said and held back a few curses he wanted to let out. He hated when kids were involved. How would this little girl cope with the loss of her parents? He couldn't imagine losing his parents, and he was an adult. "There has to be some clue here that will tell us something. Start in the office. Perhaps there is something on the calendar that will explain her absence. What information was the partner...what's his name?...able to give us?"

"He is Mr. Peter Davis. The daughter's name is Mila. She's eight years old and homeschooled. Her parents doted on her." Other than her name, the rest Lex had been able to guess from the pictures on the wall. "Cara Gallo was a teacher before she married Antony. He has a sizeable income, so after Mila was born they made the decision for her to quit her job and be a stay-at-home mother. She liked teaching and decided to keep Mila home and teach her. They did plan on enrolling her in the public school this fall so she has time to be with kids her own age. They thought it was time."

That would probably still happen. If she ended up in foster care, they would not be equipped for any type of homeschooling. "Have we searched the entire house?"

"We did a quick scan of all the rooms, but we haven't looked deep into anything. They're bagging all the evidence and taking pictures now." Craig tilted his head to the side. "What are you thinking? You have something buzzing through that head of yours. I can tell by that look on your face—you know the unfocused glaze in your eyes you get when you're trying to work through something."

He moved past his partner without answering him. His earlier idea struck a chord within him, and he couldn't let it go. What if she was still in the house? If she was...where would she hide? She was a little girl, and there were a lot of places she could crawl into. If she'd witnessed her parent's murder... That little girl needed help, and he would ensure she got the best possible.

Lex walked into the kitchen and scanned the area. He'd been careful to avoid the individuals collecting evidence and taking pictures outside of the room. Antony hadn't made it to this room, but from where his body was found, it suggested he'd been heading to the kitchen. Had he been hoping to keep his assailant from finding Mila? There was a cookie jar on the counter, but it wasn't pushed all the way back. The lid was not on completely. Had Mila decided to get a snack?

"What is it?" Craig said from behind him. "Tell me what you're thinking so I can help."

"I'm not sure yet," he answered. It was all supposition at this point. He was trying to get inside both the father and daughter's head. Lex walked over to the cookie jar and stared at it. He took a pair of gloves out of his pocket and slid them on. He didn't want to contaminate any evidence. Carefully, he lifted the lid. The jar was about half full of chocolate chip cookies, but he couldn't tell if any were missing. He frowned and replaced the lid.

"Is she hiding in the cookie jar?" Craig asked. Lex turned to him and glared. "What? You're not giving me anything. What else am I to assume?"

"Now is not the time to be a smart-ass," Lex upbraided him. "There's been a double murder and a possible kidnapping."

Craig held his hands up and said, "Point taken.

I'm going to go to the office and start looking through everything there. I'll let you know what I find."

"I'm sorry," Lex said, having a hard time hiding his frustration. "It's...I..."

"I know man. It gets to me too. Keep doing what you're doing, and we will find her."

With those words, Craig left him alone in the kitchen. He scanned the room one more time, and the only thing that had seemed out of place was the cookie jar. That could have been normal though. A last minute snack, and it hadn't been put back in place. Cara Gallo had been murdered in the office; the room Craig had gone back to search. She'd been on the floor, displayed like a work of art for the world to admire. The killer had decided to get a little creative with his dirty work, and it was disgusting. A man with that kind of signature would not have been new to the game. He had killed before. There had been ropes on the chair. Had he tied her up first, or were the scrapes on Antony's arms from them? Had he been forced to watch his wife's murder?

He should do more than stare at a cookie jar hoping it would give him answers. Lex sighed and started to open drawers hoping for anything that would give him a direction. Nothing. They were all filled with the usual things one would find in a kitchen, cooking utensils, lids to bowls, silverware. "Where are you," he said to himself.

Lex turned back to the cookie jar. He couldn't shake the idea that they were important somehow. He strolled back over to them and then kneeled down so they were eye level. Could a little girl have reached them from their normal location? He didn't think so. If she wanted them how would she get them? She could crawl on the counter, but she'd need something to climb on.

That must be it. He opened the cupboard below them and saw how she could have climbed. What would she have done if she thought she might be caught? Hide? Yes, she wouldn't want to be punished. Where would she go? He opened the cupboard on the right side, but there was no little girl hiding there. There wouldn't be any room.

There was a mixer still on the counter. Was that the normal place for it? Where would it be stored? He hadn't considered it at first, but now upon further reflection, it might not have been normal for it to be left there.

He opened the cupboard on the left of the cookie jar and inhaled sharply. A little girl sat there with two cookies lying next to her untouched. She was pale and motionless as if moving might be detrimental to her health. *God.* She must have heard or seen something. His heart shattered at how frail she appeared. "Mila," he said softly. "Can you come out here?"

She shook her head slowly and inched away from him. The trauma had taken its toll on her, and it might take a lot for her to trust him. He gestured toward the cookies. "Do you like chocolate chip?"

Mila glanced at the cookies and shuddered. He had a feeling she'd never be able to eat cookies without thinking of her parents. This poor little girl... He wanted to pull her into his arms and keep her safe always. What could he say to her to make her realize she could trust him. He had to get her out of that cupboard.

He picked the cookies up and tossed them in the trash. "There, you don't have to see them again. Can you come out here with me? I promise it is all right." She stared up at him with a haunted expression. His stomach dipped, and he felt a little queasy. He cursed in his mind, not wanting to shock her any more than she already had been. *What to do...?* "Mila, honey, please come out. No one here will hurt you."

She lifted her chin in defiance. There was a flash of something that resembled anger in her eyes. Good. She should be angry. Someone had taken something precious away from her. She would never have a normal childhood again. He'd take it all back and make it right for her if he could, but since he couldn't, he'd do the next best thing. He'd catch her parents' murderer and help find justice. He held his hand out to her. "Come with me, and I'll take you outside." He couldn't take her through the kitchen and the blood that still stained the floor. Lex would take her out the back door and to the nearest EMT to have her checked out.

Slowly, she lifted her hand and placed it in his, then allowed him to help her out. He lifted her into his arms and carried her out the back door. He didn't stop until they were in the front yard, and near an EMT. Lex set her down and brushed a dark lock of her hair behind her ear. "Are you all right?" She appeared unharmed, but he didn't know for certain.

She crossed her arms over her chest and remained silent. That didn't seem normal. Why wouldn't she talk? He had a bad feeling she'd keep quiet and they would not be able to identify her parents' attacker. He had to consider what was best for her. "Can you tell me anything?" he asked because it was his job. Lex wouldn't push, but if she could help… "What happened last night?"

Mila glanced away and toward the house. She started to shake, and he felt like an ass for making her scared all over again. "Shhh," he coaxed. "It's all right. We don't have to talk about it right now. I'm going to have the nice lady over here look you over." Mila leapt at him and wound her arms around his leg. "Don't worry," he reassured her. "I'll be with you the entire time."

He'd found her, but Mila had a long way to go before she recovered from her parents' death. Lex would do what he could, but his hands were tied. She'd probably end up in the system. God, he prayed she got all the help she needed and wasn't left to fend for herself.

CHAPTER TWO

Paige Morris blew out a breath and prayed for patience. Her daughter, Halie, had developed a stubborn streak that would drive even the strongest parent to drink. So far, she hadn't given in to the urge, but she might open a bottle of wine later that night once her precious child was asleep. One glass wouldn't hurt…

"Halie," she yelled, "if you don't come down here…"

"Geez, Mom," Halie said as she descended the stairs. She hadn't missed the eyeroll either. "Don't be so dramatic." Eight years old and an expert at sarcasm already. She'd need stock in a wine company during her teenage years if she hoped to survive them.

She pinched the bridge of her nose, trying to alleviate the headache starting to form. Paige took several breaths to calm herself. Her daughter meant the world to her, and there was a time she thought she might lose her. If her cancer ever came back… She shook that thought away. The bone marrow transplant from her Uncle Dane had worked. Halie's remission was holding strong, and had been for the past two years. "Darling," she said with the presence of calm she didn't feel. "Uncle Dane and Aunt Reese are expecting us. We should have been there a half hour ago. What was so important that we had to wait until now to leave?" It was Dane's daughter, Caitlin's first birthday, and they were having a little party for her to celebrate. Halie was excited to have a cousin—even if she was still too little to play with.

"I drew Uncle Dane a picture," she said. "I'm sorry I kept you waiting, Mom." She pulled the backpack from her shoulder and unzipped it, then pulled out a paper. "See. It's a picture of their dog, Barry with Caitlin."

Reese and Dane had recently acquired a puppy, and Halie had been begging for one of her own ever since. "It's a great likeness." It was definitely dog-shaped, but it didn't look much like a golden retriever. "Uncle Dane will love it." And he would.

He doted on Halie and always made her feel special. No little girl could have a better uncle. Especially, considering what a horrible person her father turned out to be. Thankfully, Nolan Pratt, the bastard that used his fists on Paige and smacked Halie a few times, was locked up for a very long time in a maximum security penitentiary. It was where he belonged for what he'd done, not only to her and Halie, but also to those poor women he'd terrorized and murdered. "Why don't you put it back in your bag so it doesn't get ruined. We need to leave now." She picked up the gift they'd picked out for Caitlin and handed it to her. "And please carry this so we don't forget it."

Her cell phone started to ring, and she cursed. It was probably Dane wondering where the hell they were. She snatched it off the nearby table and hit accept. "Hello," she said into the receiver.

"Ms. Morris?" a female asked. Definitely not Dane…

"Yes?" Who the hell was this? She should have checked the number before answering.

"This is Susan Miles from social services. You applied to be a temporary foster parent for emergency cases?"

She had… After she finished her teaching degree,

she'd wanted to do more for children. Especially those who had gone through something traumatic like her Halie had. She'd done a terrible job of protecting her, and she saw this as a way of redeeming herself. "That's correct," she said. "Was my application approved?" She didn't think they'd call her to inform her. Wouldn't a letter have sufficed?

"It was a couple weeks ago," the social worker replied. "We haven't mailed out your packet yet, and I must apologize for the suddenness, but you expressed an interest in helping children that experienced trauma."

"Yes," she said, "I did." Where was she going with this? Anxiety started to fill her. She checked her watch and noted the time. Hopefully, she got to the point soon. She had to meet Dane.

"Well," she began again. "Something especially terrible happened this morning. A little girl needs to be placed, and her only living relative resides in a nursing facility. We are hoping you will take her last minute."

Her heart lurched. The reminder of the terror she'd suffered at Nolan's hands flashed before her. She didn't even know what the little girl suffered, and she had gone to the worst. Had someone hurt her? "Of course. When should I expect her?"

"The head detective on the case is going to bring her to you in thirty minutes," she told her. "I needed to confirm with you first before I gave him the go ahead. I'll let him fill you in on the details. He's more familiar with the case and can answer all your questions. In the meantime, I'll get your packet in the mail today."

"Thank you," she said. "I'm glad I'm able to help."

"Have a good day and feel free to call if you need any assistance. This is going to be a tough case, so don't be afraid to reach out. This trauma…" She paused a moment. "I don't know how she'll handle it. So far, she's closing herself off. That alone will be difficult."

"All right," Paige replied. "I'll keep that in mind." Her curiosity was on overdrive. What had happened? "Thank you again."

"I should be thanking you. These things can be last minute, but this is your first placement. I do hope it doesn't scare you from trying again. Now I must go."

"Okay," she said, lost in her own thoughts already. "Goodbye." She pressed the button to end the call and turned to Halie. "I'm afraid I cannot go now. We're getting a house guest."

"We are?" she said and tilted her head to the side. "Who?"

"I'll explain later," she told her. "I'm going to call Uncle Dane and have him come pick you up instead. "Does that work for you?"

"Yes," she said excitedly.

Paige thought that might appeal to Halie. She would still get some time with her uncle, and Paige could handle the little girl coming to live with them. She wished she had thought to at least get her name.

She opened her contacts and instead of calling, shot Dane a quick text. He answered quickly that he'd be right over. She could explain to him in person. That would be much easier. "Stay here and let your uncle in when he arrives. I need to make the bed up in the guest room."

Their little house wasn't much, but she was proud of it. She'd scrimped and saved for the past couple of years while she worked and went to school. This had been the reward. A little bungalow for her and her daughter, and room to help the occasional child in need. The payments were modest, and if she needed help with any repairs, Dane was always willing to help.

This was the dream she never dared to hope for herself. Paige didn't need much and had long ago learned not to have high expectations. This was more than she could have ever dreamed. There was only one thing missing: someone, a man, worth giving her heart to, whom she could trust completely with her daughter, and allow in both their lives. She'd foolishly thought Halie's father had loved her. She'd been so blind to his faults until she had no choice but to face what a psychotic bastard he was.

She rushed up the stairs and went to the linen closet, grabbed a sheet set, blankets and pillows, then went to the guest bedroom. It was already made, but she wanted fresh sheets on it. She stripped the bed and started to put the sheets on when she heard the doorbell. Dane had been fast. She quickly finished her work, fluffed the pillow, and examined the bed. It would have to do. She grabbed the old linens and stuffed them into the hamper in her bedroom to be washed later, then rushed down the stairs to greet Dane.

Except it wasn't Dane…

The man in her living room took her breath away. He had dark hair and piercing blue eyes. His neatly trimmed facial hair made him even sexier.

She shouldn't have been paying attention to his looks, but Paige couldn't make herself look away. It had been a long time since she had been this attracted to a man, and she didn't trust it. At least she wasn't staying to her normal type...Nolan had been a pretty blond. This man was more rugged and dark—there was nothing *cute* about him. He was far yummier...

"Um," she said at a loss for words. "Can I help you?"

"Your daughter let us in," he said and gestured toward the sofa. A pretty little girl that had hair as dark as Halie's sat on the couch with her. She looked about the same age as Halie too. "The social worker said you were expecting us."

She wrenched her gaze away from the two little girls on the sofa and gave the detective her attention. "She did, but I didn't expect you this soon."

"We were closer than she realized," he offered as an explanation. "I also might have been in a hurry to see her settled." He turned toward the girls and his eyes appeared troubled, and dark circles had started to form underneath them. "She witnessed her parents's murders. The killer must not have realized she was in the house. That saved her, but I can't promise he won't try again. We're going to have a cruiser stay outside to watch the house to keep you all safe."

The social worker had left a *lot* of details out. She would have still said yes, but the dangerous part of the placement would have been nice to know in advance. "What's her name?"

"Mila Gallo," he said. "And I'm Detective Lex Foster." He nodded to the car outside. "My partner is Craig Wilson. If you need anything, contact either one of us." He reached into his pocket and pulled out a card and handed it to her. "Don't hesitate to call for anything." He smiled as she took it from him.

The door opened and banged shut as Dane walked in. His dark hair, the same shade as Halie's, was on the longer side and a disheveled mess. He tilted his lips upward when he met Paige's gaze, then turned to the detective. "Hey, Lex," he greeted him. "What are you and Craig doing here?"

Sometimes Paige forgot that Dane was a detective too. He'd been the one to bring Nolan in when he'd terrorized so many people, including Dane's wife. It also boggled her mind that Dane was Nolan's half-brother. It must hurt him a lot to realize he was related to such an evil man.

"I brought Ms. Morris's new foster child here," Detective Foster informed Dane. "Now that she's settled, I need to go back to the station to make my reports." He nodded at Paige. "Call me if you need anything or if Mila wants to talk. She hasn't said a word since we found her. The social worker thinks it'll be a while before she opens up."

"I will," she promised. *That poor little girl.*

Detective hottie nodded at Dane and then left the room. Paige stared at him as he went down her little walk and slid into the driver's seat of the car. He glanced up and met her gaze. It was perhaps her imagination, but he seemed...interested in her. Maybe he was concerned about leaving Mila with her. She had to be projecting her own attraction on to him. She mentally shook that thought away and waved at him. He nodded his head and then returned his attention to his car. When he drove off, she turned her attention back to Dane. "Halie has been looking forward to this party for days."

"So have I," he said. "Are you going to be all right?" He gestured toward Mila. "She is going to be a lot of work. Are you sure you're up to the task?"

Paige understood why he asked. No one comprehended everything Paige had gone through more than Dane. He was her oldest and dearest friend. "I have to," she said softly. "It's the only way I'll ever feel whole again." No amount of therapy had ever helped her completely. She still carried too much guilt inside of her for what she allowed Nolan to do to her, and her daughter. "I'll be fine. I promise."

"Halie," she called her over. Her daughter came to her side. "You are going to go to the party with Dane as promised. I need to stay here with Mila. She's going through a rough time because she lost her mommy and daddy. Can you be a good girl and not give Dane too much trouble?"

"Yes," Halie said. "I'm always good." She glanced up at her with a narrowed gaze as if to say how dare Paige suggest she's a naughty child.

Maybe at Dane's… "Of course you are. When you come back, can you please be nice to Mila? We need to make her feel comfortable and welcome."

"When am I not nice?" Halie lifted a mocking eyebrow. Now wasn't the time to point out when she was bratty…like this moment actually.

Paige sighed. "Can you please promise me?"

"Fine," Halie said. "I promise to be nice to the new girl."

That was all she could ask for. "Give me a hug before you go."

Halie went over and hugged her tight then looked up at Dane. "Can we go now?"

Dane chuckled softly. "Are you sure you're

ready?" Halie nodded enthusiastically. He glanced at Paige. "Are you sure you're going to be all right? I can stay longer if you wish."

"I'll be fine. There's no reason for you to stay. Truly. Go home and celebrate your daughter's birthday." Paige lifted her lips into a small smile. "Now, take Halie so I can get Mila settled. She must be exhausted."

"Very well," he said and hugged her. "I'll bring her back after dinner. Call me if you need..."

"I know," she interrupted. "I can always count on you. Now shoo."

He chuckled and called to Halie, "Come on, sprite. Barry misses you and won't stop whining until he gets proper hugs from one his favorite little girls." Caitlin had started walking and squeezed the puppy in her own version of a hug regularly.

Halie jumped up and followed Dane out the door, leaving Paige alone with Mila. She stared at the little girl with the haunted expression and had no idea what to do. Paige prayed she didn't make things worse, because if she did, she'd never forgive herself.

CHAPTER THREE

Lex scrubbed his hand over his face as frustration rolled through him. He had hit dead end after dead end on the case. So far, he had not come up with any information that would help lead him to who may have murdered Antony and Cara Gallo. He still had a few more files to read through. Craig had the physical ones on his desk, and Lex had taken the digital ones they had cross-matched. A murder like this one... It definitely hadn't been the first time the perp had killed. There had been very little trace evidence.

He clicked the mouse and opened the next file. Lex sat up and stared at the details. Another murder, another town. The detective on the case was someone he had met before too—Devlen Beck. Were the details similar…? He slid his gaze lower and read through the report. It was possible…

A family had been slaughtered in their home; the daughter had not been as lucky as little Mila Gallo. She'd been killed, tortured, before her parents. Would that have happened to Mila if she had not hidden?

He hadn't spoken to Devlen in several years. Not since they were both rookies. Lex had started in Sanville, and had only moved on to Enville when his brother, Doctor Zachary Foster, had decided to relocate. He wanted to be near the only family he had left. That had been three years ago. It hadn't taken long to move through the ranks and make detective. He'd been working with Craig for a year. This wasn't his first major case, but it was one of the most important. It would give him a chance to prove something to himself. That he could work the case and this time keep the little girl safe.

The last one…

He shook that thought away. Lex hated the reminder of when he'd messed up. It had been years now, back when he was still on patrol, but it had stuck with him. The sad look in the little girl's eyes, begging him to help. His hands had been tied then. He would have saved her, had tried to, but there had only been so much he could do. The social worker had come in, taken her from her family, then returned her a few short weeks later. They'd learned their lesson.

He snorted in disgust.

They had learned nothing. The little girl had died, and her mother and father had been the ones to kill her. The Gallo case was a little different. Mila had lost her parents and a deranged psychopath might end her life. Lex couldn't let that happen. He wouldn't.

"Any luck?" Craig closed the folder he'd been looking through. "Nothing here so far."

Lex shook his head. "Nothing solid. I need to make a call."

Maybe, if he spoke to Dev, it would help him. The case might not be the same, but it might shake an idea or two loose. He pulled his cell phone out of his pocket and flicked through his contacts until he found Devlen's name, then pressed it. He lifted the cell to his ear and listened to a few rings before Devlen's voice echoed back. "Detective Beck," he answered. "How can I help you."

"Hello, Beck." Devlen was silent on the other end, so he reminded him, "It's Lex."

"Lex," Devlen drawled out his name. "Lex the

loser who bailed on Sanville for the misery of Enville. That Lex?"

His lips tilted upward at the jab. Everyone had tried to talk him out of leaving. He might have made detective sooner if he'd stayed in Sanville. "That's not how I remember it exactly."

"Then you're becoming senile in your old age," Dev shot back. "To what do I owe the unpleasantness of having to take your call?"

His smile fell. Lex hated the necessity that garnered this call. "It's a bit of nastiness all right." He sighed. "I have a case that might connect to one of yours. I hoped to pick your brain."

Lex heard the creak of a chair. It almost sounded like Dev had been leaning back in his chair. "What case?"

This was the part neither one of them would like. "The De Lucas"

The intake of breath that Devlen took told him a lot. The case still bothered him, and the fact it remained unsolved irritated him. "That..." he was silent a moment. "It is one of the worst cases I've been assigned to. What was done to that family..."

"I looked through the notes you have on the file, and the similarities to my case is what made me think it might be connected. My case had a set of parents murdered, and by sheer luck the daughter is still alive. They were killed by a large knife, much like the De Lucas." He took a deep breath. "I was hoping you could tell me something that wasn't in the file or that you might have discovered something since the report was completed."

"I'm sorry," Dev said. "I pull the file often and read through it, but it's unsolved and I have no leads. I wish I could help. The bastard that did this...they deserve to be locked away."

Lex closed his eyes and shook his head. "It was a longshot. I had to ask."

"If you find anything…"

"I'll let you know," he finished for him. "If it's the same psychopath, it'll close both cases. They won't see the light of day again." Lex wanted to help Devlen if he could. "If you…"

"I'll call immediately," Dev answered. "I have to go."

"Later," Lex said and ended the call. It was another dead end, but something told him that the two cases were connected. Maybe he'd get lucky and solve both of them, and find justice for more than one family.

He slid his phone back into his pocket and then clicked on the next case file. The tediousness of being a detective never ended, but it was how they solved mysteries. He'd keep plugging away and pray he found the answers he needed.

"Pardon me, I was told you might be able to answer some of my questions…"

Lex glanced up and met the gaze of Antony Gallo's business partner. "Mr. Davis, is it?"

"Yes," he said with surprise in his voice. "I didn't realize you knew who I was."

His auburn hair was ruffled and his gray eyes looked stormy. It could be his grief after the loss of his business partner, but Lex couldn't be certain. "It's my job to know anyone associated with the Gallos," he told him. "What can I do for you?"

"It's about Antony's estate…" He cleared his throat. "I know this is a little crass, but my business depends on what happens with the case. They froze all of Antony's assets while the murder is under investigation. Do you have any leads or expectations on arresting anyone soon?"

"We're exploring all evidence and following all leads. I cannot comment further than that." Lex gave the standard line, partly because he didn't like the guy, and partly because it was all he could tell him. This guy bothered him, but Lex couldn't pinpoint why. In a way, he understood. His business was probably in a bit of an upheaval with Antony Gallo's murder. There wasn't much Lex could tell him, and he had no way of easing his anxiety.

"I see." Peter Davis frowned. "What about Mila? Is she all right. I noticed you located her while I was still at the house. If I noticed she'd been hiding…" He swallowed hard. "That poor, poor girl. What she must be going through."

"Mila is fine. She's been placed with someone who will see to all her needs. I'm afraid that is all I can say." His gut told him to give Peter Davis as little information as possible. Even if he could tell him more, he wouldn't.

"If she needs anything…"

"She doesn't," Lex interrupted him. "But if something does come up, I'll be sure to let you know." He wouldn't say anything at all to him. If Mila needed something, he'd take care of it himself first.

"That's all I can ask," Peter said. His voice was a little shaky as if he were fighting his grief. "I'll leave you to your investigation. Please let me know when an arrest is made. I hope you find the psycho who did this. They deserve to be locked up for the rest of their life. I wish the death penalty was an option."

"I'll keep you informed." He'd also keep his eye on him. He'd lay stakes the man was hiding something.

Peter left the police station, but the unease inside Lex didn't lessen with his exit. It gave him more to think about.

Perhaps he should go to check on Mila. It might help settle the worry spreading through him. There was also a bonus to visiting Mila—her pretty foster mother. Lex would have had to be dead not to notice how attractive the gorgeous blonde was, and he definitely continued breathing. Asking her out might cross a line, but he had been tempted. He didn't have much to offer any woman; however, Paige Morris made him wish he could.

He should call first before stopping in, but he liked the element of surprise. With that decision made, he left the station. He'd drive over and hope he didn't make the trip for no reason. Though honestly he didn't much care if it was a waste of his time. If it eased his conscience, it would be enough, for now.

ENZO STARED AT THE HOUSE. He couldn't help it. The police kept going back in and looking through it as if they'd miraculously discover all of his secrets. They'd never find any. He'd learned early on how to cover his tracks. They would only find him if he allowed it, and part of him wanted them to chase him. That would make it even more thrilling.

His phone vibrated in his pocket. He pulled it out and glanced at it, then frowned. How dare he interrupt him. Enzo punched the accept button with his finger and brought the phone up to his ear. "What do you want?"

"We might have a problem."

Enzo hated this condescending ass. "There is no problem." He'd made sure of it, and he refused to believe anything had not gone as planned.

The man let out a long draw out sigh. "I do wish you would be more reasonable. There is a problem, and since this is your mistake, I expect you to handle it."

The next time Enzo met him in person, he'd take care of the real problem. The man that hired him had to die. He was the last loose end, and then he could retire. No one else was aware of his extracurricular activities. "Fine," he said through gritted teeth. He had other things he wanted to do, and this phone call interrupted them all. "What exactly do you believe has gone wrong."

"The little girl," he said. Was he tapping his fingers? It was a soft, gentle *click-clack* that came through clearly on the phone. He must be unsatisfied. Poor little rich boy didn't get everything he wanted? Too bad. He'd live...for now. "She's still alive."

Of course she was. When he'd gone into the house she hadn't been there. If she had been, he'd have sliced her throat open and watched her blood pour out. Antony would have watched his precious daughter die. "I don't understand why you should care. You only told me to kill the man." He still didn't know that Antony was Enzo's half-brother, and he had no intention of supplying that information.

"Because she may have seen you," he said, his tone filled with exasperation. "You were sloppy."

"Don't be ridiculous." No one saw him. Ever. "If that little girl had seen me, I'd have known." And she'd be dead. He couldn't state that enough, but it wouldn't penetrate the asshole's brain. If he insisted on insulting Enzo at every turn, he'd hang up and start stalking him sooner than planned. He didn't linger in Enville only to watch his brother's house and the detectives on the case. Enzo had many reasons for sticking around.

"I would like to believe in wishes and rainbows," he began, "but I don't have that luxury. I cannot take the chance that this little girl saw you and ruin my plans. She needs to be taken care of, and you will handle it."

"You cannot order me to do anything." He stared down at his fingernails. Was there dirt under them? He'd have to clean them out. Enzo hated anything under his nails. It reminded him too much of his childhood. "If you want the girl dead, you know the cost."

He didn't do anything for free.

"You're extorting me," he said. Enzo snorted. He couldn't help himself. "I don't like it." Well, Enzo didn't like him, so in his book, that made them even.

"Then the little girl lives. That's fine with me." He pulled a small pocket knife out and opened the blade, then slid it under his nails to remove the offending particles. "If that's all, I have more important things to deal with."

"Fine," the man said. "I'll wire half into your account immediately; then after the job is finished, I'll send the other half." He didn't sound happy with that aspect of their deal. Too bad. Enzo wouldn't slit the girl's throat without proper compensation. "Don't let me down."

Enzo could use more money, and he'd happily take it before he killed the man who'd offered it to him. Why not? He wasn't a good man. Who paid someone to kill a little girl? It didn't matter much to him. A job was a job, and he'd do it either way. He never claimed to be a good man. He'd kill his niece and still sleep all right. Enzo didn't give in to nightmares. He'd lived through his own already. That didn't mean he had to allow this greedy bastard to keep breathing.

He'd get paid first, then he'd ensure the man died and in the most horrible way imaginable. "It'll be done." He ended the call and slid the phone back into his pocket. It wouldn't be the first time he'd ended a child's life, but this one would be the last. He found it distasteful. There would be no thrill or joy in it. The only way he'd have found it with Mila Gallo was if she'd been around to torture in front of Antony. She meant nothing to him otherwise.

He continued to clean his nails with the knife and stared at the house. Where was little Mila now? She had no family to take care of her. Both her parents were dead, and her grandfather was living in a senior home for the infirm. He had dementia or Alzheimer's. Enzo wasn't sure which, and he didn't really care. Maybe he'd pay dear old dad a visit soon, and tell him in detail how he'd killed his precious family.

No one would believe him. He was losing his mind.

Enzo liked that idea the more he thought about it. Maybe he would also give the police some anonymous tips as well. It would be fun to watch them scurry around like mice chasing their little bits of cheese.

First, he'd visit his father, then he'd find out where little Mila Gallo had been stashed, and after that, he'd send the detectives on the case a pretty little package. Enzo grinned. He loved being him. This was going to be so much fun. He couldn't wait to watch it all unfold. His father's dismantling would be his favorite part of it all. Maybe he'd visit him a few times. He'd need a good disguise if he planned on going in more than once, maybe even a couple different looks. He didn't want to tip the police off that much.

CHAPTER FOUR

Paige rolled out of bed and stretched her arms above her head. There were kinks in every one of her muscles. Today was the first day back to school, and she looked forward to meeting all of her new students. Teaching had given her a sense of purpose and made her feel like she made a difference. She had come a long way in the past couple of years. This was her third year of teaching second grade. She adored working with children.

If she didn't get the day started soon though, they would all be late. Halie tended to be difficult to wake in the morning. Her little angel was a hellion on a good day, but she adored her daughter. Mila had been quiet since the moment she'd come to stay with them. Nothing Paige did or said seemed to help. The poor dear was petrified and jumped at her own shadow.

She slid on her slippers and went to Halie's room. Paige opened the door and called out, "Time to wake up, sweetie."

"No," Halie called up. "It's too early. I need more sleep." She buried her head under her blanket, and all Paige could see was a few strands of her dark hair.

"I'll be back in five minutes, and if I have to I will drag you out of bed. I'm going to wake up Mila. Be in the bathroom brushing your teeth when I return, or you won't be happy with what I do." She learned the hard way she had to be stern with her daughter or Halie would rule the house.

"Fine," Halie grumbled from under the covers. "But I'm not happy now either."

Paige fought a smile. She adored the little imp. "Five minutes," she reminded her and left to check on Mila. She opened the door and peeked inside. "Mila…" Paige frowned. Her bed was empty and the blankets were on the floor. She must have had another fitful night of sleep. She headed into the room and searched for her. Mila didn't seem to be anywhere in the room. To cover all her bases she opened the closet and checked inside, then looked under the bed. Definitely not in the room…

She wouldn't panic. Mila was probably somewhere else in the house. She would go downstairs
and look there. Maybe she'd gotten hungry and went
to the kitchen for a snack. Paige stopped at Halie's
room and peeked inside. Halie stood on the other
side of the room staring at herself in her vanity
mirror. "Good, you are up. Come downstairs when
you're done dressing."

"I know what to do, Mom." The sarcasm in
Halie's voice grated on Paige's ears. She would not
dignify it with a response. Halie was never in a good
mood in the morning. This one was a little better
than others, so she'd let it go. Besides, she had to find
Mila, and she didn't have time to argue with Halie.
Paige shut Halie's bedroom door and went down the
stairs.

She checked the living room. After looking in
every corner and hiding place available, she moved
on to the downstairs bathroom, then the laundry
room, and finally the kitchen. Mila was nowhere.
Paige reminded herself to breathe. Her hands shook
as she picked up the phone and dialed emergency
services. Mila was her first charge, and it had been
less than a week, and she'd already lost her. Had she
run away? Paige hoped she was all right. What if
something bad happened to her.

"Hello, what is your emergency?" the operator asked in a no nonsense tone.

"My foster daughter is missing," she said breathlessly. Paige paced around the room as she held her cell phone to her ear. She ran her hands through her hair, uncertain what to do.

"How long has she been missing?" The operator kept up his efficient questions. How many times had he dealt with a call like this one?

"I don't know," she said exasperated. "I went to wake her this morning for school, and she's...gone. I don't know if she left or..." Paige swallowed hard. She didn't want to think of the other possibility. That little girl's parents had been murdered. What if the killer had come back and taken her? What if... She had to stop with that line of thinking and fast. If she kept on that track, she'd definitely have a panic attack.

"What's her name." The operator continued to keep his voice even and spoke with no emotion. He was doing his job, and she couldn't fault him for that.

"Mila Gallo," she told him. "She's eight years old and alone... We have to find her." Paige wasn't sure how much detail to give them. Should she tell them what she looked like? That her parents were murdered? Would any of that matter? God, she was a mess.

"I'll have dispatch send some officers out. They'll help you find her." There were a few clicks on the phone as the operator typed something. He stayed silent as he worked, and it made her even more nervous.

"Thank you," Paige said. She nibbled on her bottom lip, and her heart pounded inside her chest. Where was Mila? She didn't know how to help her, and she wanted to desperately make her feel at ease. Why would she have left? She prayed that she'd left on her own accord. "I'll wait for them to arrive."

"I'm going to end the call now. The officers should arrive soon."

Paige set her phone on the table and went to the living room to wait for the officers to arrive. She didn't know how long it would take, but she didn't know how she'd handle it until they did.

Mila was her chance to help someone and make a difference. It was not enough that she was a teacher. She wanted to really help someone who needed it, and she was already failing.

LEX STEPPED out of the shower as a text message went off on his phone. Mila Gallo was missing… He let out a string of curse words. That little girl had been through so much. He hoped she was all right. Lex dressed quickly and was out the door before he stopped to think about it. The officers that were assigned to the house were probably already helping look for her. Paige Morris had called it in. Why she hadn't thought to alert the patrol car?

Maybe she'd called on instinct.

He pocketed his phone and went to his car. It wouldn't take him long to reach the house. Maybe Mila would be located before he arrived. That would take the edge off his anxiety. Lex drove to the house and parked the car. Paige was on the porch, talking to two officers. She wore a fluffy white and pink robe and matching slippers. Her blonde hair was a little ruffled and her expression was frantic as she spoke.

She was a lovely woman. He probably shouldn't notice that about her, especially now, but he found her incredibly attractive. Lex found her desirable; however, he wouldn't act on it. He didn't want to spook her, and Mila needed her more than he did. Besides, he wasn't the relationship sort. If he was though…she'd be the perfect woman for him.

Lex opened his car door and took several long strides until he reached the front porch. Paige glanced in his direction and then rushed over to him. He pulled her into his arms on instinct. "She's going to be all right." Her scent drifted upward; honey and vanilla filled his nose. He loved holding her, and part of him wished he had the right to do more. Lex wanted to kiss her and find out if she tasted as wonderful as she smelled.

Paige stepped back and nodded her head several times. Tears fell down her cheeks. Lex wiped them away with the pad of his thumb. "I'm so sorry," she told him. Her voice was shaky as she spoke. "I said I would keep her safe, and I already messed up."

"You did no such thing," he reassured her. "Have you searched the house completely?"

She nodded. "I looked everywhere I could think of. She's nowhere inside."

"Did you check the kitchen cupboards?" He should have told Paige about where they had found Mila after the murders. Maybe she found the kitchen and the cupboards safe.

"No," she said and frowned. "Wouldn't she have to move things around to get inside a cupboard? I would have noticed something out of place."

"Perhaps," he said. "Why don't we check anyway." His gut told him that they'd find her in the kitchen.

"All right," she said. "I already arranged for a sub to cover my class today, and Dane is going to come by to take Halie to school. So I'm free to handle the Mila situation."

As if on cue, Dane pulled his car up at the curb. He turned to Paige and said, "If you don't mind, I'll go search the kitchen, and you can talk to Dane and see your daughter off."

"Okay." She glanced in Dane's direction, then turned back to Lex. "I'll be in shortly. This won't take long."

Lex nodded and then turned toward the house. He'd search the kitchen, and hopefully Mila would be there. If she wasn't, he didn't know where she could be. He hated the idea that it could be much worse than a little girl hiding because she was scared. If the same psychopath that had killed her parents came after her... He wasn't sure if he'd handle that well.

He went into the kitchen and studied the cupboards. They weren't as large as the ones in Mila's home. There was one though that was large enough and probably would easily accommodate a little girl. He didn't know what Paige usually stored inside there or if Mila had to move anything to climb inside. He went over to the cupboard and opened it.

Inside, curled into the fetal position, was Mila. She had stacked several bowls and squeezed herself into the space with them. Instead, of removing items, she made the cupboard work for her. The poor thing.

"Mila," he said. "Can you come out for me?" She turned toward him. Her blue eyes seemed even larger than he remembered, and there were dark circles under her eyes. Had she slept at all? He would have to ask Paige how well Mila had been sleeping. Lex didn't want to question her care; however, something wasn't right with the little girl. He held out his hand to her. "I promise its safe. Do you trust me?"

She nodded her head and placed her hand in his. Lex helped her out of the cupboard and then pulled her into his arms. She leaned her head on his chest and sighed. "I have you," he told her. Lex carried her out of the kitchen and stopped in the middle of the living room. Paige opened the front door and gasped.

"Oh, thank heavens," she exclaimed. "You found her. So was she in the kitchen like you suspected?"

"Yes," he confirmed. "I am going to take her to her room and settle her in. She needs some sleep."

"I'll show you the way." Paige gestured for him to follow. They went up the stairs to Mila's room. He laid her on the bed, and Paige picked up the blankets. Once Mila was settled, they both left the room

"Do you think she'll actually sleep?" Paige asked. She nibbled on her lower lip as she worried over Mila. He liked that about her...that she truly cared about the little girl entrusted to her.

"I hope so. She's clearly exhausted." He ran his fingers through his hair. "I'm afraid she might do something similar to this again. You might want to install an alarm of some sort to alert you to her movements. They have rugs or mats that have sensors in them, or even a motion detector of some sort can be installed."

"I'll look into my options. I don't want to wake up and find her missing again."

He glanced back to Mila's room and then returned his attention to Paige. "If you need help shopping for the system or installing it, call me. I want to make sure Mila stays safe."

"I'll keep that in mind," Paige said. She was still nibbling on her bottom lip. He wanted to kiss her. It was wrong of him to consider the action when she was clearly worried over Mila. Kissing her wouldn't help the situation, and he had to stop thinking of her that way.

"Call me if she needs me," he said quietly. "She trusts me, and I think it might help her if I stop by every now and then. Is that all right?"

"Of course," she agreed. "Anything to help Mila."

He nodded and then left her alone. If he stayed any longer he might do something he'd come to regret. Paige hadn't given him any indication she was interested in him. Lex had to keep reminding himself he didn't want a relationship, and Paige Morris was the type of girl a man settled down with.

CHAPTER FIVE

The walls of the psychiatrist's office were a pale yellow trimmed in light blue with tiny white daisies along the edges. Paige stared at the flowers and wished she found them comforting. They were certainly pretty, and dainty, but they didn't set at ease the nerves rolling inside her stomach. This was Mila's first appointment with Dr. Marlee Adams.

Paige and Halie had several sessions with Dr. Adams after the incident with Nolan, and it had helped them deal with their trauma. If anyone could help Mila, it was Marlee Adams. Something had to work... Mila continued to remain silent and sullen. After she'd hidden in the kitchen and scared Paige half to death, she'd started counting the days until

Mila's first appointment with the psychiatrist. They had been sequestered in Dr. Adams' office for forty-five minutes. Another fifteen and hopefully they would emerge with some progress.

The door to the doctor's office opened, catching her attention. Paige glanced up and met Detective Lex Foster's gaze. He was as gorgeous as she remembered. Her heart skipped a beat. She took several breaths and reminded herself he wasn't for her. No man would be. She had made progress in her own sessions with Dr. Adams, but not enough to accept the idea of a romantic relationship. "What are you doing here?" she asked him.

He shoved his hands into his pockets and rocked back on his heels. It was endearing, and she wished she wasn't so attracted to him. "I wanted to check in with you and see how Mila is doing." Lex nodded toward the door. "She still in with Marlee?"

Paige frowned. "You're on a first name basis with Dr. Adams?"

He shrugged and went over to the seat across from her and sat. "She's dating my older brother. We've had a conversation or two."

"Is that so?" She leaned back in her chair and crossed her arms over her chest. He had said it so casually as if he hadn't dropped news that unsettled her. She hadn't made the connection to his name before this moment. "Your brother is Dr. Zachary Foster?"

"It is," he answered. "You know him?"

"Yeah, you could say that." He'd been instrumental in saving Halie's life. He was one of the doctors on her case while she fought Leukemia. "I actually have to take Halie to see him next week for her three year checkup."

Lex frowned. "Your daughter has cancer?"

"Had," she clarified. "Dane donated bone marrow, and she's been in remission for a few years now, well, nearly that anyway." Between Halie's illness and Nolan's abuse, they'd had a long battle to fight to get where they were now. Sometimes, she still had nightmares about it all. "You look nothing like your brother." Dr. Foster had dark blond hair and Lex's hair was brown.

He laughed. "We're half-brothers. Zack looks more like his mother, and I look more like my father. It happens."

"That's true," she agreed. Dane and Nolan were half-brothers, and they looked nothing alike. Halie's coloring was more like Dane's, and it had made Reese, Dane's wife, believe he was her father at first. She didn't feel like sharing that information with

Lex though. "You shouldn't get your hopes up that Mila suddenly begins talking. She is unlikely to start after one session." It had taken Halie at least three to start opening up, and Paige even longer. She'd known she needed the therapy, but had still been reluctant to open those wounds willingly.

He scrubbed his hands over his face and sighed. "I know I am stumped. I want to catch the bastard that murdered that poor little girl's parents, but I keep hitting dead ends. If I don't catch a break soon, I'm afraid I'll never discover his identity." Lex flipped his hand forward. "She's the only hope I have left at this point."

Paige swallowed the lump that had formed in her throat. She wanted the murderer caught, but if Mila was all he had left... "I hope you find something soon. Mila has a lot to work through and you can't depend solely on her. She won't be able to handle that pressure."

"Don't worry," he reassured her. He smiled softly, hoping it eased her concerns. "I won't let her know she might be the key to solving anything. She's a little girl, and I want her to work through her trauma and hopefully find some way to find happiness."

"I think that's what we all want," she said softly.

"Helping children like Mila is why I decided to become a foster parent." She had a lot of guilt for the stupid decisions she'd made when she got involved with Nolan. The only good thing to come out of that relationship was her daughter.

The door to Dr. Adams' office opened, and Mila stepped out followed by the psychiatrist. There was a slight frown on Marlee's face, and Mila kept her gaze on the floor. "It's all right," Marlee said to her. "We can talk later…when you're ready."

Mila walked over to Lex and crawled into his lap. Paige was glad in that moment that he'd come to the appointment. The little girl seemed comfortable with him, and she'd have to talk to him about coming by to see her more often. He might be instrumental in helping her through her issues.

"Can you stay with her while I talk to Dr. Adams?" she asked him.

"Of course," he said. "She's safe here with me."

Paige went over to Dr. Adams. "So?"

"She didn't say a word the entire time. I'm afraid this is going to take a while. I did get her to draw a few pictures, but they won't help with Lex's case. I want to see her twice a week."

"I'll set up the appointments with your secretary." *Poor Mila…* "Is there anything I can do?"

She glanced over at Mila and then back at Paige. "She seems to like Lex. I'm going to talk to him after you leave and have him spend time with her. She seems comfortable with him, almost relaxed. She wasn't that way once in our session." Marlee frowned. "Keep being there for her, reassuring her, and in time she'll be open with you. In the meantime, don't lose hope. She'll work through it."

Paige nodded. "All right." At least with Marlee wanting to talk to Lex she wouldn't have to. "Thank you."

She walked over to Lex and Mila and held out her hand. Mila reluctantly crawled off Lex's lap and placed her small hand in Paige's. They walked out of the office in silence. Paige waved goodbye to him before she closed the door behind her. Paige wasn't certain about Mila, but she had a lot to think about, and she suspected so did the little girl by her side.

LEX COULDN'T LET GO of the frustration rolling through him. He didn't blame Mila. He'd be the biggest ass in the world if he did. That didn't mean irritation didn't find its way inside of him. He had to find some kind of clue...anything. The guy who'd killed Mila's parents couldn't be that good. Surely he had messed up in some fashion.

"You can't let it eat at you," Marlee said.

"Can't I?" He lifted a brow. "My job is to solve mysteries, and this one continues to stump me." He had nothing left to work with. If Mila didn't have anything to add, then he feared he'd have to give up and mark this a cold case. There was no trace evidence at the scene, and the security system had been turned off. Lex still wasn't certain if the Gallos had turned it off for some reason or if the killer had the skill set to do it himself.

Marlee walked over and hugged him. She stepped back and tucked a stray brown lock behind her ear. Her soft coffee-colored eyes were filled with concern. "Quit thinking so hard. Take a break, go talk to Zack. He needs some time away too. He is going through a rough patch with a patient. A little boy is very sick, and he's afraid the treatment isn't working. It might do you both good to spend some time together."

Zack worked with cancer patients of all ages. He'd often said the kids were the hardest. "I can stop by his office later and ask him to have lunch with me. You're right. I could use the company, and it's been a while since we spent some time together."

"Good." She rubbed his arm. "Also, about Mila…"

He lifted a brow. "Yes."

"She's taken a liking to you. If you can promise me you won't talk to her about the case right now, I'd like for you to spend some time with her. I already told Paige this, and she seemed all right with it."

"Why would she be against it?" He was not a bad man, and he was on the case to find Mila's parents murderers. "I told her I'd check in on her from time to time."

"Of course you did," she said. "But Paige…" Marlee frowned. "She has a past that I cannot discuss with you in depth. All I can say is to be careful with them all. That's bound to be a houseful of skittish females."

Lex was curious, but he didn't press the issue. He had a feeling he knew why Paige might be nervous around him. The Nolan Pratt case had made head-lines, and while he didn't know all the details because it was before his time in Enville, he had enough information to hazard a guess. Almost everyone in town knew the details of the case, and when Lex had taken the detective position, he'd read the basics in the file. He had been curious, and reading old files helped to sharpen his skills. "It's going to be fine. I promise. I will call her and schedule times to stop in so I don't surprise them."

"That's a good idea," Marlee said. "Now, go visit your brother. My next appointment will be here soon."

"All right." He chuckled. "Thanks for the advice."

"You're welcome," she said and then grinned. "I'll be sure to send you the bill."

He shook his head and left the office. Lex really liked Marlee, and he was glad his brother had found someone to make him happy. Sometimes, it made him wish for something similar in his life. He had to remind himself that he didn't really want a relationship when that mood struck him. He loved his brother, and at least one of them had something meaningful in their life.

ENZO STARED at Detective Lex Foster as he exited the hospital. He'd been trailing the pretty blonde lady and Mila Gallo, but stayed after they left to see what the detective was up to. He had plans to send him something…special. He wanted to see his mouse run through the maze and hit another wall. The blond man with Lex Foster was talking animatedly. What was their relationship? He might look into it, and if possible, use that to his advantage.

His phone buzzed in his pocket. Enzo pulled it from his pocket and glanced at the screen, then frowned. His employer was calling. Probably to harass him and wonder why he hadn't killed Mila Gallo yet. It hadn't been difficult to locate the little girl. He kept tabs on the detectives assigned to the case. It amused him to toy with them before he skipped town. The police had led him straight to the doorstep of his niece's foster mother. That didn't mean he was in any hurry to kill Mila. Enzo liked to take his time, and his employer could stew a little longer. The bastard was far too impatient. Enzo worked on his own timetable, and he refused to do a sloppy job. If he wanted to do something right, he had to do it slowly.

He shoved the phone back in his pocket and glanced toward the detective. One day soon, when Lex Foster returned to work next, he'd have a stimulating package. One that would make his head spin, and maybe even fill with excitement. At least until he realized that it was another dead end. Too bad he wouldn't be able to see his face when he opened it. Perhaps it was time to find a way to watch when he toyed with the police. He had a friend who specialized in computers and had taught him a few things. Enzo might have to use his limited knowledge to his advantage. He silently saluted the detective. His lips curled into a devilish smile.

Let the games begin...

CHAPTER SIX

T he school day had been a trial. It had been a couple weeks since Mila's first appointment with Dr. Adams, and she still hadn't talked. It was starting to frustrate Paige. At least school gave both Mila and Halie something to occupy their time with. She was grateful Halie was in the other second grade classroom. Registering Mila had gone well, and they agreed to place her in Paige's classroom. She had wanted her there so she could monitor her progress and be able to tell Dr. Adams if she adapted or not.

Paige loved teaching and was glad she'd decided to get her degree. Helping children had become her passion, but some days she questioned her sanity. She was still acclimating to her new class and learning all their names. There were two boys that had seemed to make it their lives' missions to drive all the adults in the school crazy. She'd lost count of the number of pranks the little…dears had orchestrated in the first week. There were some teachers that might use a stronger word to describe them; however, Paige believed in positive thinking. She wouldn't compare them to all the nasty things others did. Maybe with enough patience they would realize how much their actions hurt others. At least she hoped so. Either way she would have a conversation with the boys' parents. Something had to be done to curb their troublesome behavior.

She glanced in her rearview mirror at the girls in the backseat. Paige wished willing Mila to talk would work. Her appointments with Dr. Adams didn't seem to be emanating as much progress as Paige had hoped. She had another appointment in two days. Lex was growing impatient with the lack of evidence in the case. He came by several times a week to visit with Mila and hoped each time she'd talk to him and open up his case with more details. Every time he left more disappointed than the last. His frustration was becoming more and more evident on his face. He was due to come by again soon, perhaps even that evening. Paige prayed it went well, but she doubted it would. Nothing was going right lately.

"How are you two doing back there?"

"We're fine," Halie answered. "Can we have ice cream when we get home?"

Of course, Mila didn't say a word. She barely glanced up either. The poor thing… It broke Paige's heart to see her so forlorn. "No ice cream," she told her daughter. "It'll ruin your dinner."

"No, it won't," Halie replied mulishly. "I'll still eat whatever you decide to make." She narrowed her gaze. "What are we having for dinner anyway?"

"I was thinking spaghetti." She hadn't thought about dinner and had forgotten to pull anything out to make. Spaghetti was something she could make easily enough. She could defrost the ground beef in the microwave. "I have the stuff for a salad in the refrigerator too, and maybe some garlic bread."

"Can we have ice cream for dessert at least?"

Halie was not going to let go of the idea of ice cream… "I'll think about it." At least she wasn't throwing a fit about the idea of spaghetti. Sometimes she would fall into a tantrum that made Paige wish her ears didn't work. She pulled the car into the driveway, put it in park, then killed the engine. "All right, everyone out and head to the porch." She pulled the keys out of the ignition, grabbed her bag, and exited the car. Both girls were on the porch waiting for her to unlock the door. "Put your backpacks in your rooms. We will work on homework after dinner." She pushed the door open, and both girls went inside. Mila moved slower than Halie, but she didn't fight Paige on anything. At school, she followed the rules and did her work, but didn't socialize. The other kids sometimes pointed at her, but at least they didn't pick on her. Paige had worried they might and it would send Mila several steps backward. Mila went right to her room and put her backpack away. Both girls came down the stairs when they were done.

Halie jumped around and clapped her hands. "Can I watch TV?"

"Sure," she said and kissed her forehead. "But first, I need you to pick up all your toys in here and put them away." Paige turned to Mila. "Do you want to watch TV with Halie."

Mila nodded her head slowly. At least that was a response. It was more than the little girl had given when she'd first come to stay with them.

Halie tilted her had to the side and asked Mila, "Will you help me with the toys?"

Mila stared down at the toys scattered across the

living room floor. Several dolls, a stuffed teddy bear, toy cars, and a ball. Paige had no idea why her daughter had brought them all out of her bedroom, and really didn't care. Mila didn't answer Halie verbally. Instead, she leaned down and picked up the teddy bear and hugged it to her chest. Paige fought tears.

"You like him?" Halie asked.

Mila nodded and squeezed the bear tighter.

"Her name is Elsa," Halie told her. "She's a polar bear, and she doesn't mind being cold." Her daughter shrugged. "Seemed like a good name for her. Would you like to keep her?"

Mila snapped her head up and met Halie's gaze. *How sweet...* Paige was glad her daughter had a good heart. Even when she drove her crazy, she never doubted that. How would Mila respond? She clearly liked the bear and wanted to keep her. "It's okay," Halie said. "You don't have to talk." She went over and hugged Mila. "You keep Elsa if it makes you feel safe."

Halie had wanted ice cream for dessert, and Paige intended to do one better. She'd take them out to her favorite place and let her pick out whatever she wanted. After dinner, she would surprise them with the special treat.

"Finish picking up the toys," Paige said. "I'm going to start dinner."

She swallowed the lump in her throat and fought the tears that threatened to fall. Mila was making progress. Perhaps it wasn't as fast as Lex would like, but at least she would be able to get past the trauma. In time, she might be able to talk about it. If that was years down the road, so be it. What was important was Mila and her ability to live her life. Finding the person that murdered her parents was important, but Paige fully believed, if given the choice between justice and their daughter's mental health, they would have chosen what was best for her.

That is what she would have wanted for Halie anyway. She left the girls alone and went into the kitchen. Dinner wouldn't take too long, and she wanted to give the girls some time alone. Halie was the one who would manage to get through to Mila first. They trusted each other…

LEX PULLED his car into the driveway and stared at the house. He wanted to go in and check on Mila, but didn't want to disturb them. The attraction he felt toward Paige was becoming a distraction he couldn't afford, and Mila was pulling at his heart-strings something fierce. He wanted to do right by that little girl, and his failure was eating his insides raw.

He sighed and got out of the car. No time like the present to make that ulcer grow inside his stomach. All right, he probably didn't have one, but at the rate he was going it wouldn't take long for one to form. He crossed the lawn to the front porch and rapped his knuckles against the door. When it opened, he didn't find Paige on the other side. Instead, her daughter, Halie, stood on the other end.

"Hello," she greeted him. "Are you here to see Mila?"

Lex pasted a smile on his face. No need to scare another little girl. She was a darling, and he liked Halie a lot. She resembled her Uncle Dane and even had a similar dimple in her left cheek. Lex liked Dane, and it helped him to feel a little at ease with Halie and Paige. "I am. May I come in?"

"Yes," she said. "But only because my mother told me you can be admitted whenever you stop by. Otherwise, I'd have to say no." She placed her hands on her hips. "Uncle Dane said never to let anyone in the house that is a stranger."

"Surely I'm no longer a stranger to you." He lifted a brow.

She narrowed her gaze and then looked him up and down. "I don't know you, so yes, you are. We may have met a few times, but you're not family."

Lex fought a grin. "That is definitely true. Your Uncle Dane is right. Don't let any strangers in." He gestured toward the door. "I'd suggest not even opening it. Next time yell through the closed door or get a stepstool to look through the peephole. You can never be too careful."

With the person that murdered Mila's parents still unknown, he liked the idea that Halie didn't open the door to strangers. It would go a long way to keep everyone inside the house safe. They still didn't know for certain how the killer had gained access to the Gallo house. Lex didn't want to process another murder scene, and if it had to be the females that lived in this house... He shuddered at the thought. He'd grown attached to them all in the past few weeks.

"Girls..." Paige stopped short when she noticed Lex lingering at the front door. "I didn't realize you were here. How do you feel about ice cream?"

He shrugged. "It's good. Why?"

"I promised them a treat from Snowberry. Would

you like to accompany us?" She looked gorgeous. Her blonde hair was slightly messy, and her cheeks had a nice rosy hue to them. Lex wished he could pull her into his arms and kiss her. What would she do if he acted on the impulse?

He hadn't eaten anything since lunch. Lex should probably get some real food, but he didn't want to say all that to Paige. "I could eat." Maybe they had something less dessert-like at the store. He doubted that, but he'd make do.

"Good." She grinned. "Perhaps you would like to drive then too."

He'd rather he drove then Paige. Lex liked to be in control when he could and hated relinquishing it to anyone. He could keep an eye on them all while he was with them too. "Fine by me."

Paige clapped her hands. "Who's ready for ice cream?"

Halie jumped up and down. "Me, me."

Mila sat on the sofa hugging a white bear for dear life. Lex smiled at her and leaned down in front of her. "Do you like ice cream?"

She nodded and squeezed the bear again. Still, she didn't speak. What would it take for her to say something, anything? Lex blew out a breath and attempted to ease the frustration inside of him. She was a little girl, and she'd lost so much. He couldn't force the issue. They had to let her come to them, be comfortable and trust they would keep her safe. There was no telling how long that would take. He stood and held his hand out to her. "Then let's go pick some out." Hopefully she would be able to indicate what kind she liked because it was clear she wouldn't come out and tell them.

Lex rubbed his hands together. "I'm excited for this ice cream. Let's head out." Maybe he'd actually eat some.

Halie shot out the door and ran to Lex's car. Paige shook her head and laughed. Mila reluctantly set her bear down on a nearby chair then placed her hand in his and glanced up at him with expectations he wasn't sure he would be able to meet.

Paige walked next to him as they headed to the car together. Almost as if they were a family... That was a weird thought, but he couldn't shake how right it seemed to feel. They were not his to claim, but a part of him wanted to be able to. With his job, he didn't think he could have something like this. He saw too many marriages fall apart. Dane and Reese seemed to truly love each other, but he had doubts even they would make it in the end. They both had very high profile careers. How did they handle a small child with all they had going on in their lives?

He shook all those thoughts out of his head. That line of thought would lead nowhere. There was no family in his future. If his brother ever married Marlee, perhaps he'd be an uncle, but kids of his own... He didn't think that was possible.

CHAPTER SEVEN

Ice cream had been the best idea. Of course, it wasn't hers, but Paige didn't believe in semantics where family outings were concerned. Halie had devoured her chocolate marshmallow, and somehow managed to stain her white dress with it. Mila actually had a smile on her face. She was almost beaming, and that happiness warmed Paige's soul. That was why she'd wanted to foster children in need. It helped them; as well as, eased the need inside of her to do something good. This, in her opinion, was exactly that…good.

"You're smiling," Lex said. "Do you like ice cream that much?"

She turned to face him. He had an adorable look on his face. It was a mix of befuddlement and interest. Lex Foster was such a gorgeous man. Her heart skipped a beat, or several... Keeping count was near impossible to do. Paige could easily get lost in the depths of his deep blue eyes. He made her feel things she thought long buried. She cleared her throat. "I do like ice cream, but that's not what is making me smile."

He glanced at the girls and lifted his lips into a smile. "She's come a long way."

"Not nearly enough, but yes, she has." Paige fully intended to be there for her every step of the way. Mila may have lost her parents, but she didn't have to face the demons by herself. "Even the smallest bits of joy help. Dr. Adams doesn't hurt either. She's really good with her."

"Marlee is an exceptional therapist." He tapped his fingers on the table. They had brought their ice cream outside to enjoy the late summer weather. "I am a little biased considering she's dating my brother and I like her a lot, so you don't have to take my word for it."

"You're right," she agreed. "I don't." She could tell him she had her own experiences with Dr. Adams. Both she and Halie had gone through extensive therapy, but she didn't think this was the time to mention it. Divulging her personal history would be too much, too soon. They barely knew each other. He might be privy to the casefiles involving Nolan Pratt and how he terrorized not only her and Halie, but Reese and Dane as well as murdering some not so lucky women.

Nolan was a psychopath she sometimes wished she had never met. The only thing worth having out of that relationship was her daughter. For her alone she couldn't completely regret her past. She did often wish she'd made better choices once she realized she was pregnant. Nolan should never have had a place in Halie's life. She couldn't erase that choice from her past, but she could make better ones for their future. "I'm capable of making my own judgment of her skills. As it happens, I do agree with you. She's a wonderful therapist."

He grinned. "I suppose that is at least one thing we can agree on."

She lifted a brow. "Are you keeping a list? Do you expect we will be in each other's company that much you need it to fall back on?"

"Maybe," he replied nonchalantly. "I am not certain how long this case will take, and I hope to keep things congenially between us while Mila is in your care."

She jerked back. "Is she going somewhere?" Did

he know something she didn't? Did the social worker assigned to Mila's case think that Paige was doing a terrible job? Would they place her in someone else's care? They couldn't do that... Mila was finally starting to thrive. If they moved her, she might take some major steps backward.

"No," he said and waved his hands a few times. "That's not what I meant at all. I have no idea what the long term plans are for Mila's placement. She's doing well with you, so I don't foresee them moving her anywhere." He sighed. "I'm sorry I misspoke. I should have said that as long as the case is open I'll have to make a connection with her. One day she might be able to tell me something that will be instrumental in locating the bastard that murdered her parents." He glanced over at the girls to make sure they weren't listening, then turned back to her. "I need to be more careful when I speak. I don't want to spook her or let them overhear something that might disturb them."

She lifted a hand to her chest and took several deep breaths. Paige had been terrified for a brief moment that Mila was leaving them. She hadn't realized how attached she'd become to the little girl. If it were up to her, Mila would never be taken away. She had come to mean a lot to Paige in the short time she'd lived with her and Halie. Mila was swirling her spoon over the melted chocolate chip ice cream in her bowl. Halie had finished hers a while ago and had started to twirl around in circles. She had too much energy. "I don't think they're paying much attention to either one of us." That was good. It would have been bad if Mila had heard any of the tail end of their conversation. Paige hoped when she was ready to speak she'd come to one of them on her own. She didn't want her to feel forced into speaking. "We should probably take them home. They still have a little homework to finish and Halie needs a bath."

"I'll round them up," he offered.

She smiled. "Thank you."

Lex stood and walked over to the girls. Halie continued to twirl her little heart out. Mila glanced up at him and smiled. She really did like the handsome detective. Maybe it was because he'd been the one to find her after her parents were murdered, but Paige suspected it was more the man himself. He was really good with the girls, and would probably be a wonderful father in the future.

It was too bad she couldn't be his other half. Some woman was going to be lucky to call him hers one day. He managed to get Halie's attention and directed them to the car. Paige sighed and stood to join them. Their leisure afternoon was at an end, and she had her work cut out for her when they arrived back home.

LEX COULDN'T STOP THINKING about Paige, more importantly what it would be like to kiss her. The more time he spent in her company, the more he became fixated on her. He didn't need this obsession with a pretty blonde with quite kissable lips. His heart couldn't take the constant thundering. He'd never been so drawn to a woman in his life. It was making his conviction difficult to remain single permanently. He wanted more with Paige, more than he believed he should have. He didn't know if she'd even accept him in her life, so all his musings might be moot anyway.

He pulled the car into her driveway. After he had it in park and the engine was off, the girls unbuckled the seatbelt and practically ran from the car. It was good to see Mila acting a little more like a child, even if her sadness was still evident when she smiled.

"They seem a tad anxious to get inside," Lex said as he stepped out of the car.

Paige shrugged. "I can't fathom why, but you know how kids are. Pockets full of energy us adults wish we could tap into."

Lex didn't know much about children. He would have to take her word for it. He was ten years younger than his brother, and in some ways had grown up as an only child because of it. They were close, but not in the way brothers closer in age might be. Zachary had been away at college when Lex was still in elementary school. Lex had been a surprise baby their parents hadn't expected later in life. "Is it all right if I stay a while longer? I'd like for Mila to become more comfortable around me."

That would make things easier when she was finally ready to speak, but that wasn't the only reason he wanted to stay. Lex wanted to spend more time with Paige. He'd never admit that aloud though. He couldn't shake his feelings for her, and it was time for him to explore what they meant.

"Sure," she said. "You can help them with their homework." Her grin had an evil tilt to it. "They're second graders. It shouldn't be too difficult for you."

"Right," he said. Something told him that she

planned on being highly amused at his attempts to help them. "What is their homework exactly?"

"Mila is in my class, and Halie is with the other second grade teacher." She sighed. "My daughter is a bit temperamental. For the benefit of her learning environment, it was decided she didn't need her mother as her teacher." She glanced at the girls who were still bouncing around on the porch like Tigger on a high. She was right…it would be amazing to bottle that energy. "I requested Mila be placed in my classroom. I wanted to keep an eye on her." She took a deep breath. "So, to answer your question, I have no idea what Halie brought home with her. Mila shouldn't have much so she's the easier of the two."

"I'll help them both." How hard could it be? "You can relax and have some peace and quiet for a while." That might endear her to him a little bit. Lex still wasn't certain he wanted a relationship of any sort, but he believed in keeping his options open.

"All right," she said. "I do have some work I need to go through. It would be nice to get it done earlier than normal for a change."

"Then its settled," he told her. "You work, and I'll be on homework duty."

They strolled to the porch. Halie still jumped around, but Mila had settled on the porch swing and leaned her head on the arm. "It's about time," Halie said in a long drawn-out tone. "You were taking forever."

Paige glanced up at him. "You certain you want to tackle this task?"

"I can handle drunks, both mean and touchy-feely. Two little girls shouldn't be able to undo me." He prayed his statement wasn't all bluster. Lex had never dealt with girls. Women, yes, but they had wanted the attention he offered. Mila and Halie might purposely make his life difficult. He fully intended to assist them whether they liked it or not.

She held up her hands and laughed. "Have it your way. Shout for me if you run into difficulties."

Paige pulled her keys out of her purse and unlocked the front door. She pushed it open and screamed. Lex stepped in front of her in an attempt to protect her. "Keep the girls outside," he ordered.

He pulled his phone out of his pocket to call for a forensic team, and his partner. This was not a good sign. The polar bear Mila had clung to was shredded in the middle and stained red. He hoped it wasn't blood, but honestly it didn't matter. Mila would be devastated, and only one person could have caused this. The killer was watching them. He didn't know why or what the purpose of destroying the little girl's bear could be. "This is Detective Foster. I need a unit out to 1366 Pinecrest Lane. I also need you to contact Detective Craig Wilson and have him dispatched to the same address."

"Affirmative," the operator replied. "Will there be anything else?"

"A CSI team," he said. "There's been a break in, and I need them to gather as much evidence as possible."

"Done," the woman said.

"That is all." Lex ended the call and turned to Paige. She was shaking.

"He was in my house."

God. He wanted to pull her into his arms and ease her worries, but she had every right to be scared. The man who had destroyed that bear had killed Mila's parents. He was more than capable of doing much worse than tearing a bear apart and covering it in red dye. The murderous bastard wanted to frighten them, probably more than that. What game was he playing?

He cursed under his breath.

"It's not safe here," he said, frustration reverberating in his voice. "I don't think you should be here alone. Sending a patrol car by periodically isn't enough." Where the hell had it been when the perp had entered the house?

"What do you suggest?" Her voice shook as she spoke.

What options did they have? He could have them moved to a safe house or… "I'll move in with you." Lex couldn't believe the words came out of his mouth. He couldn't very well take them back. The more he thought about it, the more he liked the idea. "For now, I think we should find a hotel for the night or you can stay at my place. They're going to be a while processing the scene."

Her face had gone ashen. The girls, thank heaven, had stayed back when Paige had screamed. If Mila had seen this… She was making progress, and this was sure to set her back. "I can go stay with Dane," she said. "But I agree. I don't want to be in the house alone. If you don't mind sleeping on the sofa, I'd be more comfortable having you around."

"Good. Call Dane and make arrangements for tonight. Have him come here to collect you and the girls. I don't want you to be alone for one second."

She nodded and reached for her cell. He rubbed his eyes, trying to erase what he'd seen. He had to find the psycho before he caused even more irreparable harm.

〜《♡

Enzo cackled from the shadows. They had found his gift. If only his little niece had been the one to find it. He wanted to hear her screams. It would give him so much pleasure... Ah, the sound of terror. The pretty blonde lady had delivered at least. When they had left earlier, he'd seized the opportunity to enter the house and examine it for clues. Mila clung to that polar bear as if it had been a lifeline, and perhaps it had been. Enzo didn't know why she liked it, but he cured her of the affliction. She should be void of any comfort. When he killed her, she would find nothing but relief in death. It would be his gift to her.

The detective appeared frustrated. He loved watching the police squirm. They were chasing their tails, and he'd be long gone before they found even the smallest clue of who he was. He was too good at his job. After Mila's life was snuffed, he only had one task left to complete. He'd visit his father one last time and deliver his killing blow. Not true death, but the death of his family line. Whatever remained of his father's mind would be destroyed, and he'd be lost to those memories forever. He deserved to suffer for all he'd done. Enzo could have had a better life, if he'd had a better father.

The last laugh would be his…

He stared at the house and saluted them from his hiding place. "Thanks for playing, little mice. We will all meet soon." He might even kill the blonde lady and her little brat. It would be quite enjoyable to play with the woman before he left Enville for good. She was a beauty, and he might relish becoming… acquainted with her. "Soon, my lovelies. Soon…" He always kept his promises, and this time would be no different. They would all feel the sharpness of his blade. He wasn't quite done with the game yet though. He still had that special gift to send to the detective. Enzo planned on ensuring that was delivered in the next couple of days. He couldn't wait to see what the detective did after he received it. This was so much fun…

CHAPTER EIGHT

Paige stared at the online order on her phone. She had to order a brand new polar bear for Mila. They had been lucky, and Mila hadn't seen the one torn apart and covered in red. As attached as the poor girl was to that bear in such a short time though... Paige had to replace it. She had been calmer and even a little happier since Halie had given Elsa to her. Paige might not be able to bring her parents back, but she could give her the one thing she found comfort in since Mila had lost them.

"What are you doing?" Dane asked.

"Placing a rush order," she replied and pressed her finger to the phone. Cost was not a concern... only getting that polar bear as fast as possible.

"For what?" he asked. His tone filled with confusion. "What could you possibly need that has to be delivered that fast?" She held the phone out so he could look at the screen.

"Don't say a word," she warned him. "I am trying to do this without any fuss."

He nodded solemnly. "I don't think you should return to your house. It is clearly not safe."

Paige glanced toward him and shook her head. "Don't start. I am not going to let that evil bastard control our life. I am going home, and nothing you say is going to change my mind."

She understood why he was concerned. A madman had entered her home and left an unpleasant surprise. Paige intended to take that threat seriously, but she refused to let him win. She would install a better security system, or Lex would. They had discussed it before she left for Dane's, and Lex had stayed behind to supervise the investigation. He had been insistent, and she didn't want to argue with him in front of the girls. Besides, his reasoning had been sound. Paige hated the idea of anyone invading her space again. It would be hard enough to return home knowing the killer had been there. So she agreed Lex could pick up the new system to install after the forensics team was done processing the evidence left at her house. When she returned, it would be ready for them. Hopefully it helped to deter the bastard. Paige really didn't want to leave her own home. She would if she had to, but she'd put that off until there was no other choice left.

Dane sighed. "I wish you would listen to reason."

"I am perfectly reasonable," she replied mulishly. "You're being overprotective." She met his gaze. "I understand you feel responsible for me and Halie, but we are going to be fine. I promise. Lex is going to be staying with us, and I've taken precautions. No one is going to hurt me or the girls." She finished placing the order for the bear and shoved her phone into her pocket. The delivery should be there when they returned home. The cost for next day delivery was astronomical but worth it. "I need to wake the girls so they can get ready for school."

Dane clamped his hand on her arm and stopped her from moving. "I don't think that is a good idea."

"Why ever not? They'll never be ready in time if I don't wake them soon." She yanked on her arm. "Let go."

"Please," he begged. "Call in to work for the day. Your class will be fine with a substitute for a short time. You don't know how determined this person is and what he might do to get to you."

"He knows where I live," she said, exasperation

filling her voice. "The school would be safer at this point. At least it has more security. No one is getting inside that building without proper identification."

Dane frowned. It was almost adorable. "You might be right."

"There is no *might* about it. I am," she chastised him. "Besides, you don't really want me here. You and Reese don't need me and the girls around. It has to be disrupting your schedule, and Caitlin will be better if we're not here too. This is your time to be with each other without having the responsibility of other people. Enjoy it."

He blushed. Damn it, why did he have to be so endearing. "Fine. But I want you to know that if you need to come back you are always welcome. I love you and Halie, you're my family."

Paige stepped over to him and embraced him in a tight hug. "I love you too, you big oaf, and I know if I need you I can always depend on you." Dane was her best friend. She couldn't imagine a life without him in it. That didn't mean she had any desire to take advantage of his generosity. She stepped out of his arms and tilted her head to the side. "You're good people. I'm lucky to have you."

"Yes, you are," he said with a hint of amusement

in his voice. "If you want I'll wake the girls and you can finish getting ready."

"That would be wonderful." She grinned. "Halie is a bear, and it will be nice to have one morning not dealing with her."

"Ha, ha," he said, good naturedly. "I do have one request."

"Oh?" She lifted a brow. She was almost afraid to find out what he wanted. They had gotten through his concern about going to work and returning home. What else could there be?

"I'd like to drive you to work."

"And how will I manage to get home if you do that?"

He held up his hand. "Hear me out before you nix the idea."

"Fine," she grumbled. "But I'm not promising anything else."

She really hated depending on anyone, and she liked the freedom having her own car would give her. Paige really didn't want him to drive her anywhere.

"I can drive you in to work and Reese can return your car to your house. Lex can pick you and the girls up after school is out. I talked to him…"

"Excuse me," she interrupted him. "The two of

you decided for me and thought I'd go along with it and not put up an argument?" Paige couldn't recall the last time she was this angry. "No."

"You're not going to listen are you?"

"I'm not. While I appreciate your concern, I can manage to drive to work without incident. I don't think it is necessary for you or Lex to drive me anywhere. Now that we have settled that, why don't you go wake the girls?"

Paige didn't give him time to respond. She was perhaps being a little hard on him, but if she didn't stand up for herself, no one would. After she'd escaped Nolan, she promised herself she would never be a doormat again. If things escalated to the point she'd need a ride to work, she'd arrange for a substitute instead. At that point they might need to consider the safe house option. For now though, she fully intended to live her life without any changes.

LEX SAT in his car outside Paige's house waiting for her to return from work. He had been tempted to follow her home, but decided against it after he had a long conversation with Dane. The last thing he wanted to do was push Paige into refusing any security. She might not want him to stay with her if he overstepped. Lex needed to stay with her. If she wouldn't consider a safe house, this was the only other option left.

He tapped the steering wheel impatiently. Where was she? Lex picked up his phone and checked the time. She should have been home by now. It wasn't more than a twenty minute drive from the elementary school to her house. Should he go look for her? No. He'd give her another ten minutes. Maybe there was some unexpected traffic or it had taken her longer to finish her after-school routine. Either way, he shouldn't panic...yet.

Paige's car turned on to her street, and he breathed a sigh of relief. His heart couldn't take much more of this. They had to find the killer as soon as possible. He hated he might not be able to keep Paige and the girls safe. It had killed him when they had found that bear decimated. He didn't know what Paige had told Mila and Halie about the incident. He'd have to follow her lead until he had a moment to talk to her about it all.

Lex waited for her to have the car in park and all of them to exit, then he stepped out of his and joined them. Paige nodded at him. "Sorry we're late; you must be worried."

"Not at all," he said. "I figured you were delayed." Lex didn't want to spook her.

"You're right. I had to talk with Halie's teacher. She was...difficult today." She blew out a long drawn out breath. "She knows something happened, but I didn't know what to tell them. Halie loves Dane, but we've never all packed up and stayed with him, and the police all over the house before we left only made her more apprehensive." Mila had withdrawn more and, if possible, seemed quieter. She'd been making progress, and this might have set her back. He hoped not... Marlee would have to be informed as well. The doctor would need to know how to handle Mila's next appointment.

"If you want, we can discuss what to tell her later," he suggested. "It would help me to know what I should or should not say in front of the girls." He hated not being in control. It was driving him a little mad that he couldn't dictate the situation, but he had to follow her lead.

"That is a good idea," she agreed. "We can talk while they're doing their homework. They don't have a difficult assignment and should be all right on their own. Both classes have the same worksheet to do." She grinned. "Unless you want to attempt to help them. You were denied the opportunity yesterday. I'd hate to deprive you of that experience."

He shook his head. "I'll have to save that joy for another day. I think our discussion is more important. Did they have any trouble with their work at Dane's?"

"No," Paige said, then sighed. "Mila worked in her usual silence, and Dane helped Halie. He has a lot of patience with her and since Halie adores him, she doesn't usually give him too much difficulty." She glanced in the direction of the girls, then back at him. "I suppose I'll get them started and then we can talk. It shouldn't take long."

"Sounds good."

They walked together on to the porch. Both girls waited for them on the swing. A package sat by the door. He picked it up and held it to her. "Are you expecting something?"

"I am," she said, then whispered, "a new bear for Mila."

"Ah," he mouthed the word. "Good call."

He pulled out the new keys. "I should have given these to you already. Unlock the door and step inside, then I'll show you how to disarm and rearm the security system." Lex had stayed overnight in the house and cleaned up after he installed the new system. It gave him a chance to make sure the system worked and get more acclimated to the house. He needed to have a good understanding of his surroundings in order to protect the girls better.

Paige did as he suggested and then they went inside. He went over the schematics of the system and waited for her to familiarize herself with it. After they finished with that, she took the package and carried it into the kitchen. "Girls, go work on your homework," she called to them on her way. Lex followed behind her.

"I thought we would have more privacy in here," she told him.

"Will they do their homework without supervision?" He frowned. When he was younger, he would stare at his homework without doing it for a long time. It usually took his mother coming in several times for him to finally complete it.

"They should. It's a math coloring sheet. Halie likes math and coloring, it's in her zone. I'm not certain what Mila likes, but she hasn't been difficult so far, and I don't expect that to start now."

"Good." He would still check on them later. "About what we should say to them…"

"I think we should keep it simple. Tell them we had a robbery maybe. Mentioning the bear or that it might be the person who killed Mila's parents might cause her to backpedal."

"A break-in isn't exactly a lie either..." He frowned. "I wish we didn't have to tell them anything at all. I still cannot believe he broke in and destroyed that bear. You do realize what this means, don't you?"

"He's been watching us," she said so softly he almost didn't hear her.

She walked over to him, and he pulled her into his arms. "Ssh," he said when her tears started to fall. "I'm here. Nothing is going to happen to you or the girls."

He wished he could wrap them all in bubble wrap, or better yet, the best bullet proof material available. There was only so much he could do. She lifted her head and met his gaze. Her cheeks were still wet from her tears, but they had stopped falling.

"I'm sorry," she said. "I tried not to break down, but it hit me like a freight train at full speed. This isn't the first time I've dealt with something like this. I thought I could handle it."

"No one blames you, least of all me, for giving in to your fears. It's normal. If you need to do it again, don't let anything stop you. There's nothing wrong with crying every now and then."

"I hate giving in." Her lips wobbled a little.

Lex wanted to erase that hurt from her eyes. There was only one way he knew to do that. He leaned down and pressed his lips to hers. It was a mistake, but one he refused to regret. Sparks ignited between them, and it was the lightest of touches. He wanted to deepen the kiss but stepped away instead. That one taste served to only intensify his craving for her.

She stared at him, bewildered, then lifted her fingers to her lips. Paige turned away from him abruptly and went to the package. "I should open this and give Mila her new bear. She sliced the box open and she pulled out the bubble wrap, set it on the table, glanced inside, then gasped.

"What is it."

Her hands shook as she met his gaze. "This is *not* the bear I ordered. It's..." She swallowed hard. "A bloody knife. I don't know what happened to the bear..."

He cursed and pulled out his phone. What were the chances the blade in the box was the one used to murder the Gallos? "Don't touch anything else. Go check on the girls. I need to make a few calls."

"Are we going to have to leave again?"

"No," he said. "Not this time."

She nodded and left the room. It was going to be another long night. This might be the one thing he needed to break open the case. Perhaps the killer wasn't as smart as he thought. If it was the knife that he used on the Gallos, it might have important trace evidence on it. At least he hoped so... He would hate it if this only terrorized Paige more.

CHAPTER NINE

Paige sat in the living room, staring out the window in the dark. She'd tucked the girls into bed a couple hours ago. Somehow, she had managed to get Mila to sleep without her bear. So far she hadn't asked for it, but she would need a ready excuse for its disappearance. Maybe she could blame the police? No, that wouldn't work. What reason would they have to take it, other than the truth, that would put her at ease? None. She'd have to tell her something though...

Maybe she'd get lucky and she wouldn't ask. Though Paige's luck hadn't been the best of late, so she wouldn't count on that. She had contacted the company, and it hadn't been shipped yet. They apologized and refunded the shipping cost. Paige wished she hadn't been so distracted when she opened the other box. If she had looked at it more closely, she might have realized it wasn't from the place she'd ordered the new bear. At least it would arrive soon and Mila could sleep comfortably with her new friend. This was her second night without the bear. As long as she had it before the third night, Mila might not question it. Not that she talked...but still... Paige sighed. It was a mess.

The police had come and gone, taking the bloody knife along with the box it had been in. Lex was still in the kitchen making phone calls. He'd been busy dealing with the new evidence and seemed to almost forget Paige and the girls. That was all right. At least, she kept telling herself that. Part of her wished she had stayed at Dane's and never found that stupid knife.

She didn't want to be alone...

Lex had to work. It was his job to find the Gallos' murderer and keep them safe. She didn't want to interrupt that; however, her unease grew exponentially with each passing second. What if he was out there now, watching them...? She shivered uncontrollably.

"Paige?"

She glanced up and met Lex's gaze. What would

he do if she rushed to his side and threw her arms around him? Would he hold her? Kiss her again? She shook those thoughts away. He was there to protect them, not start a torrid love affair. Still, she couldn't help wondering why he'd kissed her in the first place. What had he hoped to gain, and did he actually want something more with her? "Yes?"

"I didn't realize how late it was," he said. "How long have the girls been asleep?"

"A while," she answered. "Did you need something?"

"No," he said with a shake of his head. "I don't know. I'm anxious. It's almost as if we're getting close, but I feel like this is a trick of some kind. Why would he send that blade here? There has to be a reason. The bastard didn't leave any evidence we could use behind, and he willingly sends what could potentially be the murder weapon here? There is no way it is the one he used to kill the Gallos."

Paige wished she could help him solve this. She wanted nothing more than for the killer to be found. All of this was starting to bring her past trauma to the surface. She thought she could handle it, but it was starting to become clear that might not be the case.

She should book an appointment with Dr.

Adams. When she took Mila to her next session she would. They were scheduled for another session in the morning. It was a Saturday, so at least there was no school as well. She didn't think she'd be able to teach a class in her current state of mind. "You're probably right," she said. "He's toying with us all, but I don't understand why."

"I don't either," he replied, the frustration evident in his voice. "But there is little we can do tonight. What time is Mila's appointment tomorrow?"

"Eleven," she answered. "She's Dr. Adam's last appointment before lunch."

He nodded absentmindedly as he paced the room. "Do you think we should reschedule it?"

"Absolutely not," she said adamantly. Mila needed those therapy sessions. She was making so much progress, and Paige feared if she missed any it might hurt more than help. "We're not cancelling or rescheduling anything."

"It might not be safe…"

"Of course it isn't safe," she shouted. "Nothing and nowhere is safe. It won't be until you find the person tormenting us." He jerked a little as if her words were a slap to the face. She threw her hands up in the air and kept talking. He had to understand why they couldn't skip Mila's session with Dr.

Adams. "Are we supposed to stop living our lives in the meantime? Mila is going to her appointment, and she is going to take one more step toward getting better. We are not going to allow that man to take anything else from us."

Lex rubbed his hand over his face. "All right." He took a deep breath. "We will go, but I don't think we should all go. We can call Dane to come here and stay with you and Halie, and I'll take Mila to her appointment."

"No," she disagreed. "I need to be there. I do agree about calling Dane. I'll have him come pick up Halie. I'll feel better if she stays with him for a few days."

She should have left Halie there to begin with. Paige had vowed never to put her daughter in danger again. How stupid was she? When she took Mila in, she actually thought it would be fine. Even when she was warned that it might be precarious. Mila's parents were murdered. How could she have expected a different outcome?

"If you want, I can call Dane."

"I'll do it." She shook her head. "It's my daughter, and I want to take care of the arrangements." Paige would not give up what little control she had left. "I'll do it now."

Her hand shook as she reached for her phone.

Lex reached over and placed his hand over hers "It can wait. Call him in the morning. It's late and you don't want to disturb him."

She lifted her head to meet his gaze. Paige turned toward him and laid her head on his chest. He wrapped his arms around her and held her close. Paige shook uncontrollably. All the times Nolan had hit her, when she feared for her life, the moment she almost lost everything…it all came rushing back. She couldn't do this. The strength she thought she had didn't exist.

"I'm going to do everything I can to find the bastard, I promise," he said.

"I know." Her voice wobbled. "Fear doesn't always have reason to it. What makes me scared isn't completely about the person who murdered Mila's parents. I have my own past that comes back to haunt me from time to time."

He ran his hand over her hair. "Do you want to talk about it?"

"Not particularly," she said. The last thing she wanted to do was lay herself bare to him. This strong, gorgeous man who had a protective streak longer than she could imagine. "I would rather forget everything even when I know it isn't possible." She stepped out of his embrace and met his gaze. There was one thing that would help her forget...even if it was only for a little while. "Kiss me."

LEX STARED at her for a moment, stunned. Had he heard her correctly? "What?" He blinked several times, but she was still there in his arms, and she'd asked him to kiss her. Should he? She'd been clearly upset, and he didn't want to take advantage of her.

"Kiss me," she said again. "Not a peck on the cheek or a light kiss like we shared earlier. I want a real kiss. One that we both know we want and need."

Lex didn't stop to think. He bent down and pressed his lips to hers. She wanted a kiss, and he fully intended to deliver exactly what she requested. The kiss started light, like a tease that would explode into something spectacular. Then it went deeper, longer, and got hotter with each roll of his lips over hers. She moaned, and he took advantage of it. He pushed his tongue into her mouth and tangled it with hers. It was a dance of desire, and his blood was on fire for her. He wanted much more than a kiss. He wanted, no needed to strip all her clothes off and kiss every inch of her delectable body.

Had he lost his mind?

They shouldn't be doing this at all, but he couldn't stop. Didn't want to stop. He should. Lex lifted his mouth from hers. Somehow, he had found the strength to. He stared down at her eyes. They were glazed over with a passion that matched his own.

"Kiss me again," she demanded.

"Are you sure you want to do this?" He had to be sure. Lex didn't want her to regret her decision come morning.

She met his gaze boldly. "Are you always this talkative when a woman asks you to kiss her?"

"Only when it means something." He took a deep breath. "If you don't really want me, want this, then we have to stop."

He might be losing his one chance with her. The one he didn't realize he wanted until this moment. Lex kept women at a distance, but somehow this one woman had come to mean more to him than he thought possible. If she hadn't taken Mila Gallo in he might not have gotten the chance to know her. In a twisted way, he owed the murderer for opening his eyes to the possibility of being with Paige. He'd never admit that aloud though.

"I want you," she told him. "I've wanted you since

the moment we met, but I was too afraid to start something new. I'm tired of being afraid." Paige lifted her hand and pressed it to his cheek. "Don't make me wait anymore."

"Never again," he promised and leaned down to kiss her again. This time it was gentle, and coaxing. He pulled her close and cupped her ass in his hands. Paige rubbed against him, and this time he groaned. God, she was sexy. He picked her up and she wrapped her legs around him.

"Take me upstairs," she said. Her voice was breathy as she spoke. "My bedroom will give us the privacy we need."

Lex did as she instructed. The last thing he wanted was to be interrupted. It was always a possibility with two small children in the house, but he hoped they didn't wake. He wanted Paige and hoped to make her crazy with desire before they came together completely.

When they reached her bedroom he pushed the door open, then kicked it shut lightly with the heel of his foot. He turned around and pressed her to the back of the door. Lex trailed kisses down her neck and down to her breasts.

"I need you naked," she demanded. "I want to feel your skin against mine."

"God, yes," he agreed. He swung her around and set her to the floor. "First, this dress has to go." It was a practical black dress that she had worn to work. He didn't know why, but he found it incredibly sexy. He spun her around and gradually unzipped the gown, kissing her shoulder and back with each slow pull of the fastener. When it was down all the way, she shimmied out of it and it pooled at her feet. She stood in front of him in a lacy bra and panty set that made him harder than he'd ever been in his life.

She looked over her shoulder and said, "Your turn."

He'd taken off his tie earlier when he'd been on the phone with his partner, Craig. The collar was open wide. She undid the buttons and pressed her hands to his bare chest, then pushed his shirt and jacket off at once. "That's better, but we're not quite there yet."

He lifted a brow. "No?"

"No," she affirmed. Then pulled on his belt buckle. "You're not nearly naked enough."

He groaned as she slid her hands into his pants and cupped his cock. She stroked the length over and over again until he thought he'd burst with pleasure. "You need to stop or this will end before we have a chance to truly begin."

"We wouldn't want that," she said and pulled her hand out. Then she pushed his pants down. Paige glanced up and down appreciatively. "You, sir, are gorgeous."

"So are you," he told her. He pulled her into his arms. "And I plan on making you moan with pleasure."

"Promises, promises," she teased.

He didn't answer her with words. The best way to prove to her he could keep his end of the bargain was to show her. He unhooked her bra and slid it off, then sucked one of her pert nipples into his mouth. She moaned. Lex moved over to her other breast and gave it equal attention. After she was shaking with need, he set her on the bed and pulled her panties off. "Now to kiss you all over the way I wanted."

Lex settled between her thighs and kissed her clit. He pushed his finger inside of her and stroked as he sucked on her. She moaned again and started to squirm. He repeated his actions until she climaxed. Lex licked her one last time and then glanced up at her. "Do you have a condom." He wished he'd thought to ask before. He was so hard it hurt.

"In the drawer." She pointed. He got up and

found the package inside. He pulled one out of the box and came back to her.

"Let me," she said and took it from him. She opened it and then slid the condom over his hardness. He groaned at her touch. "Now, come inside me."

He picked her up and moved her across the bed then settled between her thighs. "Are you ready?"

"Oh, yes, please." Her words were music to his ears. This was what he'd wanted since the moment he met her. He'd been denying himself the pleasure of being with her, knowing her, and touching her in every way possible. Lex was glad he'd finally given in to the temptation, and now, he'd finally be able to love her in all the ways he'd imagined.

Lex pushed inside her. He'd never felt anything as wonderful as being inside of her. She wrapped her legs around him, and he began to rock inside of her over and over again. Lex lost all ability to think. All he could do was keep moving until she climaxed again and drove him over the edge. When his release hit, he nearly blacked out from the sheer pleasure of it. When he came to his senses he rolled off of her and disposed of the condom, then joined her in the bed again. He wrapped his arms around her and held her close, and silently vowed to never let her go.

CHAPTER TEN

Paige rolled over and hit a warm body. For a moment, she had forgotten the night before, but once the memories started flooding in, her body heated with need all over again. It was a decadent and pleasurable night in his arms. She wanted to have many more nights like that, with Lex. How could one person come to mean so much in such a short time? She wanted to be with him every day if possible. It might be a ridiculous desire, but it was what she felt.

His eyelids fluttered open, and he met her gaze. Her lips tilted upward into a sinful smile. "Good morning, sleepy head," she greeted him. "I'm having a fabulous morning so far. How's yours?"

The corner of his mouth twitched slightly. "It's

better than most I've had. I wouldn't mind exploring ways to make it even better."

She lifted a brow. "I'm listening." Paige snuggled into him. "Tell me more about how we can...explore."

He wrapped his arms around her and snuggled her to him. Her body came alive in a tingle of energy ready to explode. The right touch would put her over the edge. Lex slid his hand down her back, and he cupped her ass, then squeezed lightly. She barely suppressed a moan. He was very good with his hands, and his tongue. He'd made love to her several times the night before. Each time, her climax was more explosive than the one before. Lex continued to amaze her with his skills. "We could start with a little foreplay right here." He dipped his head lower until his lips met the crook of her neck. Then he trailed his tongue over a particularly sensitive area. This time she couldn't control her moan. "Do you like that?"

"Yes," she said breathlessly. "What are we going to do? Get all hot and bothered and then...nothing?"

"Oh, no," he reassured her. "I'd never leave you unsatisfied. I have plans. Lots and lots of plans, and all of them involve us both being naked, and completely sated."

Paige giggled. Giggled! Like an innocent girl with

her first lover. In some ways, he was. Nolan had been a controlling, abusive monster. He took his pleasure from her and didn't bother to ensure that she was pleasured. This was nothing like she'd ever experienced before. She wanted to wrap them in a time bubble that no one could interrupt. Unfortunately, reality had a way of sneaking in and ruining the best moments in life. Still, she fully intended to take advantage of the specialness of this new budding relationship and store the memories for further examination later. "I'm yours to pleasure as you will." She continued to be surprised by him and could not wait to find out what he would do next.

"I will take that generous gift and ensure you are never disappointed in giving it to me," Lex whispered in her ear. "Let me show you what you can expect from me when you choose to allow me into your bed." He trailed his fingers over her belly and down to her entrance. Lex touched her clit and caressed it until she began to squirm in his arms. He pushed one finger inside her and stroked as he rubbed his thumb over the sensitive nub. "That's it. Let go."

She was going to scream. If she did it might wake the girls. The last thing that Paige wanted to do was have that kind of interruption. Halie was inquisitive and would ask so many questions. Ones she definitely did not want to answer. Paige opened her mouth about to give into the urge. Before a scream could erupt from inside of her Lex pressed his lips to hers and kissed her. It distracted her enough that, when her climax hit, it shook her so much she nearly screamed with pleasure.

Lex lifted his head and met her gaze. "I have one question for you."

She stretched languidly like a cat ready to curl up and take a nap. Paige could easily fall back to sleep and have the best of dreams. "What?"

"Do you want to join me for a shower?"

Paige considered it. A shower with him would probably be the most decadent thing a woman could experience. "That sounds divine," she began. "But I don't think we'd come out as clean as we should."

"Darling," he said huskily. "You'll be the cleanest you've ever been when I'm done. I can promise you that. I plan on washing every inch of your delectable body. I'll pay so much attention to every part of you, there will be no doubts."

She groaned. "You're a dirty, dirty man."

"But you love it." God, did she...

Paige rolled to her side and slid her leg over him.

"Love me now, and we shower alone. Make it fast and hard. I need to feel you pounding into me."

Lex let out a sound she could only describe as a combination of anticipation and desire. He reached over her to the box of condoms and grabbed a packet. He opened it with his teeth and pulled it out, then skimmed it over his hard length. "Are you ready?"

"Always," she said.

He pushed inside her and did as she asked. His cock glided into her with one thrust of his hips, and he continued to rock inside of her so fast she almost forgot to breathe. She dug her nails into his back when her climax began to climb. When she was about to scream, she leaned down and bit his shoulder. He pushed into her several more times and went over the edge. Her body shook with pleasure, and she couldn't wait to find time to have sex with him again.

When her body started to calm down enough she asked, "Do you want to shower first?"

His words came out a bit breathless. "You go ahead. I need a few more moments to unwind."

She untangled herself from him, albeit reluctantly, and rolled out of bed. She stood before him completely naked and unashamed. She stopped at the entrance of the bathroom and then glanced at him over her shoulder. His gaze was trained on her every movement. She flashed him a sultry smile and then said, "If you want, I suppose you can join me. It might be fun to be as clean as you promised."

Paige went into the bathroom and started the shower. He strolled in and shut the door behind them; his lips tilted upward into a sensual smile that sent shivers down her spine. This was going to be the best shower of her life, and she couldn't wait...

LEX DROVE to Marlee's office. Mila remained quiet in the backseat, and Paige emulated the silence by staring out the window. She hadn't said much after their self-indulgent morning shower. The night they had spent together had been phenomenal. He enjoyed it so much he hoped they would repeat it again, and again, and again. He'd never tire of loving her.

He loved her...

That didn't scare him as much as he thought it would. It was the kind of love that existed without question. He couldn't stop feeling it if he wanted to, and he couldn't deny it or shut it out of his heart.

Lex accepted that he'd always love her, and no matter what, she would forever be a part of his life. Sometimes love was inevitable, and his feelings for Paige were exactly that.

"Here we are," he said as he pulled into a parking spot. "Are we ready for this?"

Mila nodded. Paige met his gaze and smiled. "Do you think it is safe to exit the car?" she asked.

Lex glanced around him and made sure no one was around. Well, no one suspicious. If the killer was out there, Lex wasn't sure he'd recognize him. He hated that he hadn't found the bastard yet. He wanted to make sure Mila, Paige, and Halie remained safe. "All clear," he said. "I'll escort you inside, then I need to make a few calls."

"Calls?" Paige lifted a brow. "About?"

"I need to see if the forensics report came in from the..." He glanced over his shoulder and thought better of finishing that sentence. Mila still didn't know about how her bear was destroyed, and her new bear was supposed to arrive soon.

"I understand," Paige said. "Let's go inside.

They exited the car and walked into the office together. Lex kept his focus on their surroundings He didn't want any surprises to spring out and catch them off guard. He had to keep them safe. Maybe if he kept repeating that to himself he'd be able to complete that task. Lex had never been so frightened of losing someone in his life. His heart had never been this involved.

When they entered the office, Marlee's secretary was busy typing away at the computer. She glanced up and greeted them, "Welcome. Dr. Adams is finishing with her previous appointment. Take a seat and she will be with you shortly."

"Go make your calls," Paige said. "We'll be fine. No one is going to attack us here"

He hoped not... "I won't be long."

"Don't worry." Paige lifted her lips into a soft smile. "Go work. We need you to do your job."

Lex nodded and left them alone in the office. He didn't want Mila to overhear any of his conversation. He lifted his phone out of his pocket and called in to the station. After three rings someone finally answered, "Hello."

"This is Detective Alexander Foster." He rattled off his credentials to her, and then asked, "Did the forensic reports come in on the Gallo case?"

The only sound he heard was typing as fingers flew across a keyboard. He could almost see the image inside his head. After a few moments, the woman who answered the call said, "The report on the knife came in without any concrete information. The knife didn't have real blood on it and no prints or other evidence." She was quiet a moment. "The bear did have a strand of hair. They couldn't get any good evidence on it. The hair was dark."

Hair... It could be Halie's or Mila's, but it also could be the killers. "Send the reports to my e-mail." It was more than they had before, and he'd take it. What other lead did he have?

"It's done," she answered. "Is there anything else?"

"No," he said. "That's all I needed. If anything else comes in, contact me or Detective Craig Wilson immediately."

"Will do," she answered, then hung up.

He checked the time on his phone. The call hadn't taken more than fifteen minutes. He could call his partner and update him. No, he'd do that later.

His phone started to vibrate. Lex looked at the caller ID and frowned. It was an unknown number. He clicked the accept button, "Detective Foster," he said into the receiver.

"Detective," a man's voice filled his ear. "This is Peter Davis. We spoke in your office the other day." The business partner...

"Yes, I remember. What can I do for you, Mr. Davis?"

"I was wondering if you made any progress in your case?"

The man sure was persistent. Was the murder really affecting his business that much? Lex had been slacking on investigating Antony Gallo's business. Perhaps his murder was tied to it somehow. He'd call Craig and have him do a deep dive into the financials and see if there was a motive for his eagerness. He repeated what he told Mr. Davis in the office. "We are exploring all evidence and following all leads."

"Yes," Mr. Davis said. "That's what you said before. But has there been any progress?"

"There isn't much I can tell you. No arrests have been made." They didn't even have a real suspect. "Is there anything else I can assist you with?"

"What about Mila?" He seemed awfully concerned about Mila...

"Mila is still doing fine," he reassured him. "You need not worry about her welfare."

"Good, good," he said. "You will call me if anything changes?"

He might do more than call him if he had

anything to do with the Gallos' murders. "You can count on it."

"Thank you," Mr. Davis said. "I won't take any more of your time. Have a good day, and I hope you find the murderer soon."

"So do I," Lex replied and then hung up. He didn't want to talk to him more than he had to. He pocketed his phone and then went back into the office and sat next to Paige. She leaned her head on his shoulder, and he wrapped his arm around her. This was where he belonged. He would protect Paige and the girls. He had to.

IT WAS a beautiful day to create chaos. Enzo would be making his move on Mila soon, but first he had to spend a little quality time with his dear ole dad. It wouldn't be as much fun if he couldn't deliver the news of his granddaughter's impending death in person. Enzo had waited until the perfect time to visit the facility where his father was receiving care. It was a busy place with an employee turnaround that might make a person's head spin if they paid close enough attention. That was good for Enzo though. They wouldn't question a new face. He had the uniform down pat and a fake badge to pin to his shirt. He'd chose the nondescript blue-green scrubs to wear for the visit. It would not be good to stand out or catch anyone's notice.

He whistled as he walked toward his father's room. The bastard had a private room. That would also be useful for this interaction. He didn't need any witnesses. If all went well, he'd be in and out with no one the wiser. Well...except his father. Enzo hoped to leave a lasting impression on him.

Silently, he stepped into the room. His father sat in a chair near the window, gazing outside. He almost looked serene, and perhaps he was, but Enzo didn't much care either way. Enzo stayed near the door and studied him. His father's hair had gone completely gray and was streaked with white. He couldn't see his whole face; however, the wrinkles were still evident near his eyes.

Enzo moved into the room and closed the door behind him. It was time to have his chat with his father. The old man turned toward him and narrowed his gaze.

"Antony?" he said.

"Try again," Enzo drawled and strolled over. "I'm the unwanted one."

"Lorenzo?" His voice shook as he spoke that one word. "What are you doing here?"

Anger surged through him. "I see you're not as feeble minded as they said you were. Clearly, you recall your bastard child."

"It's…" The old man swallowed hard. "I can't erase my mistakes. What's done is done."

Enzo grinned evilly. "Didn't they tell you the good child died? Your dear Antony is no longer amongst the living." He wanted to drive the knife in deep. "And soon little Mila will join him in the after-life." He wanted his father to feel pain. As much as he could possibly dish in one harsh blow.

"Noooo," his father moaned. "Not Antony. He's not gone. You have to be lying to me." He stood and reached for him, but Enzo stepped out of his reach. His father's touch abhorred him, and he didn't want to feel it at all. "Did you do this?" the old man asked. "Are you responsible?"

His father wasn't a small man, but still Enzo towered over him. He leaned over slightly and whispered, "I did, and I'll be the one who takes Mila away from you too."

That was the last straw. Pain flashed in his father's eyes and tears fell down his cheeks. Enzo had accomplished his main goal. This was what he'd come for and now that he had achieved everything he'd set out to do, he'd finish it. "Don't worry, Father," he said menacingly. "I plan on leaving you alive. There's no point in ending your pain early, is there?" He turned and left the room, not once looking back. No one paid him any mind as he strolled out of the facility. Now there was only one thing left to do: grab Mila and end this.

CHAPTER ELEVEN

Lex had been quiet since they left Dr. Adam's office. Paige started to worry that perhaps she might have done something wrong, but if she had, she had no clue what it could have been. Their morning had gone well. Better than that, it had been fabulous. She could use many mornings like that in her future, and hoped it would be the case. Perhaps the calls he had to make had disturbed him. She didn't know what else it could be.

"Dinner's ready," she said. "Are you hungry?"

"Actually," he began, "I am."

He had taken up space in her living room to work. He had his laptop and phone on the table along with several manila folders. Probably all the information he had available on the case. Part of her was curious and wanted to look at it. She wouldn't though. The last thing she wanted to do was compromise the case in any way.

"Good," she told him. "Come to the kitchen and join us. Halie is setting the table, and Mila is helping. They both seem to be in good spirits."

"I'll be right in. I have to close my computer down and store the files."

"All right." She nodded. "Don't take too long."

She went back into the kitchen. The girls were sitting at the table, waiting for their dinner. Halie leaned over and whispered something in Mila's ear. The little girl laughed. That was the first sound Paige could recall her ever making. She'd been so quiet and sad since she'd arrived at her house. To see her smiling and laughing...it was amazing. Paige went to the counter and started placing the food on the table. They were having roast beef, roasted potatoes and carrots, fresh bread, and a simple salad for dinner. Once everything was on the table, Lex walked in.

"Something smells delicious," Lex said.

Paige beamed. She wasn't the best cook, but there were a few dishes she could do well. "Have a seat," she told him and gestured toward an open chair. Paige and Lex had seats across from the girls. Since they were getting along so well, she didn't want to separate them. Paige put food on the girls' plates. "Eat before your dinner gets cold."

"Awe, Mom, you're no fun," Halie said but then started eating without any fuss.

Mila picked at her potatoes and nibbled on them. It made Paige wonder if she'd ever had roasted potatoes before. She'd ask her later so she wouldn't make her feel uncomfortable around everyone. She wanted Mila to feel safe.

"What were you two laughing about when I came in?" Lex asked. "It sounded like you were having a lot of fun."

"It was nothing," Halie said and speared her fork into a carrot. "We were playing a silly game."

"I like games," Lex insisted. "I'd love to play with you."

Halie ignored him and continued to eat. Her daughter could be obstinate at times. "Maybe they can share with you another time," Paige said. Mila ate a carrot slowly. "Do you like your dinner?" she asked the little girl before she could stop herself.

Mila glanced up and met her gaze and then said, "Yes. I've never had it before, but I like it." Her voice was a little hoarse, almost like a whisper. Probably because she hadn't used it in weeks...

Tears threatened to form in Paige's eyes. She

spoke. Mila had finally said something. It was so simple, but it was more than she expected. Mila hadn't done more than nod or shake her head for weeks now.

"I'm glad you are enjoying it." She nearly choked the words out. Paige didn't say anything else. Partly because she didn't think she could since she was overly emotional, and she also didn't want to terrify the girl with her outburst.

Lex had gone completely still by her side. It hadn't gone unnoticed by him that she'd spoken either. She hoped he didn't push the girl. Paige knew why he needed her to speak, but if they rushed her, she might close up again. "Miss Morris is an amazing cook, isn't she?"

Mila nodded and smiled. "Yes, she is."

"She's all right," Halie said.

"Thanks for the raving endorsement, sweet pea." Trust her daughter to bring her down a peg or several. "You make your mama feel oh, so good."

Halie wrinkled her nose. "You know what I mean."

"Do I?" Paige lifted a brow. "I suppose I might."

Paige started to pay more attention to her own meal. Dinner conversation was all well and good, but she was hungry too. Now that Mila was talking, perhaps they could finally get some answers from her. It might help Lex find her parents' killer. Paige hoped so. She didn't want him terrorizing any of them. The sooner he was locked up, the better.

"Miss Morris," Mila said softly.

Paige glanced up at her. "Yes, dear."

"Can I have more?"

"Of course," Paige answered, delighted she was eager to talk and eat. She scooped more roast, potatoes, and carrots on to her plate. "You can eat as much as you want."

Lex leaned over and whispered in her ear, "I know it is too soon to ask her questions, but I wish I could."

She turned toward him and said, "I know."

He leaned a little closer and asked, "Want to have a little adult time later?"

She nearly groaned but managed to hold it back. This was not the place to talk about sex. Though the idea of stripping naked and rubbing herself all over him sounded delectable. "I might be willing," she answered. She was more than willing; she was all ready to lead him to her room and have her wicked way with him. Now she was super anxious to finish dinner and settle the girls in bed. Too bad they had hours before they could do that.

"Did you decide what movie you want to watch tonight?" she asked the girls. It was her way of reminding both herself and Lex they had promised the girls a movie night.

"Can we watch the one with the talking snowman?" Mila asked. "Halie told me about it, and I've never seen it? She said she named Elsa because of the snow queen." She frowned. "I miss Elsa. Did you find her yet?"

Paige wanted to hug her so much. "Not yet. I'm sure she'll turn up." As soon as that package was delivered... "We can definitely watch that movie though. After you finish dinner, wash up and go play. I'll call you when its time."

"Can I be excused now?" Halie asked. "I don't want any more."

"Yes," Paige said. Lex rubbed her back with the palm of his hand. She turned to meet his gaze.

"It'll be all right," he said. They both were concerned about Mila. She hated that they had to be devious about replacing the bear. The trauma would be too much for her.

Mila continued to eat her dinner. After several moments of silence, she glanced up and said, "A bad man hurt my father."

Paige and Lex went completely still. She held her

breath and Lex set his fork down. Mila was ready to talk, and neither one of them seemed to know what to do next. They were taking their cues from her.

"Yes," Lex finally said. "A very bad man." Before this moment they didn't know for sure if it was a man or a woman that had committed the murder. They could guess, but there was very little evidence to go on. "Do you want to tell us more?" Lex held his breath a moment, waiting for her to answer. This was the detective coming out. His back went straighter, and his eyes seemed to zero in on his target. Not in a menacing way, but a sharpness came over his gaze as all his focus set itself on Mila and her answers. Nothing would distract him from what Mila had to say, and he would ensure she was comfortable as she explained everything. Paige's heart hurt for Mila, and it fluttered with anticipation as she listened in silence.

"Maybe," she said.

Lex let the breath out slowly. "You can tell us anything you want. Whenever you are ready, we'll listen."

Mila pushed her food around her plate. "I wanted some more cookies. Mama said no; I'd had one, and that was all I'd been allowed. I knew the rules, but I didn't care. I sneaked and got more." She glanced up at them, her eyes glistening with tears about to fall down her cheeks. "I don't like cookies anymore."

Paige couldn't eat more if she tried. He stomach soured after that confession. She fought tears but held them back. Her tears wouldn't help Mila. "I won't make any cookies for you," she promised. Halie would have to eat cookies at Dane's if she wanted them. She would not add to Mila's misery.

"Did you know the bad man?" Lex asked.

She shook her head. "He had a different voice...he didn't sound like my dad." Did that mean he had an accent?

"You only heard him?"

Mila nodded. "I was hiding...I thought my mama would find out I sneaked cookies." A tear slid down her cheek. "I waited, and then I heard my father." It was interesting that she said *mama* and *father*. That was something to discuss with Dr. Adams. "He would have been mad too, so I stayed in the cupboard. The mean man...he..."

"It's all right," Lex reassured her. "You don't need to say any more if you don't want to."

"He was bad."

Lex nodded. "We will find him." Conviction was threaded through his voice as he spoke those four words to Mila. Paige believed him. He wouldn't let this case go until he found the person responsible.

"Can I leave?" Mila asked. "I'd like to play with Halie."

"Yes," Paige told her. "Go." She flashed her a smile, but it felt strained, probably was. She waited until Mila was gone before she turned to Lex. "Did any of that help?"

"Some," he said. "But it is not nearly enough. At least we know it was a man and he had some sort of accent, but I'm not sure where to begin."

"You'll figure it out." She had to remain hopeful. Otherwise, they might never be able to live their lives freely. She pushed her plate away and stood. Maybe cleaning after dinner would help clear her mind. She had to do something because she'd never felt so helpless in her entire life.

IT WAS A SCHOOL DAY. They had decided that they would all go. Lex would drive them and pick them up, but would continue with his investigation in the interim. It was the only way he'd agree to what he considered a logistical nightmare. After the fiasco of the bear and knife, he didn't feel comfortable letting them out of his sight. Paige didn't blame him.

Now it was lunch time. Paige looked forward to the break. Her stress levels had maxed out. Perhaps Lex was right and she should take a leave of absence and have a sub take over her class for a couple weeks. She was not doing her students any favors by being brave and sticking it out. She'd snapped at one of the more troublesome boys when she usually had more patience.

After she dropped the kids off in the lunchroom, she went back to her classroom. Usually, she went to the lounge for lunch, but she had a terrible headache and wanted some peace and quiet, if only for a little while. She nibbled on her peanut butter and jelly sandwich. It tasted like sawdust, so she wrapped it back up and put it back in her lunch box.

A knock echoed through her classroom. "Pardon me, Miss Morris," one of the recess attendants said. "Do you have a moment?"

Oh, Lord. What did one of her students do now? She was going to stop in the office before she left and arrange for that substitute. Paige couldn't take any more. "Yes. Please come in." She gestured toward the woman. She was older with shoulder-length, snow white hair, and soft blue eyes. What was her name? "…Mrs. Campbell what can I do for you?"

"It's about Mila." Her tone was a combination of agitation and trepidation.

Paige sat up straight, suddenly troubled. Her hand started to shake, but she kept it hidden under her desk. She didn't want to show anyone, especially the aid, she was scared. No one at the school knew how bad the killer had terrorized them at her home. She'd like to keep it that way if she could. "Did something happen to her?" The aid was a little nervous and played with her hands. Paige's heart pounded inside her chest. An unease settled deep inside her gut as she waited for her to respond.

"I'm not sure..." She nibbled on her bottom lip. "She was in the cafeteria, but when we went to go outside, she came up missing. I came here to see if she returned to the classroom, but..."

"No..." Her heart thundered inside her chest and drowned out all the sounds around her. There was only one person she could trust to help her and Mila. She grabbed her purse and retrieved her phone, then dialed Lex. "Come to the school immediately," she told him when he answered. "Mila's missing."

"I'm on my way," he said and ended the call.

There was something comforting in his commanding tone. It gave her courage to do what she had to. She would ensure Mila was all right. The little girl was her responsibility.

She turned to Mrs. Campbell. She didn't wait to see if the aid did as she instructed. There were more immediate concerns. "Alert the office. She has to be found."

Paige ran out of the room and went to the cafeteria. There might still be evidence there, or someone could have seen her. She couldn't wait for Lex to arrive. She had to start the search and hope she found her before he arrived. If not.... The alternative was unthinkable.

CHAPTER TWELVE

E nzo had been watching the little girl for days. It was time to finish the job. He'd visited his father for the last time the night before. Made sure to explain exactly how he intended to end his family line. The bastard might have been lucid enough to understand, but Enzo couldn't be certain. Either way, the fun had to end sometime, and now was as good a time as any. Besides, his client wouldn't quit hounding him. He had to kill the girl and leave Enville.

It was lunch recess at the elementary school. There was too many eyes, but he might be able to grab her. She didn't seem to play with any of the other kids. If he lured her away, he could do the job and dump her body in a place the pretty blonde could find her. With the detective taking residence at the house, he couldn't do it there. Too much heat, and too many cops for his liking. The house was nearly crawling with police, and he couldn't get near it without being discovered. He should never have agreed to kill the girl. Not to mention, he could have done it sooner, but that wasn't much fun. He liked to enjoy his kills. Enzo hated he had to rush this one.

The kids started to spill out of the school. So many little brats. He'd go insane having to deal with all that screaming day in and day out. Why did people have children? Enzo would never willingly father a child. He hated kids. Had absolutely no use for them.

Mila stepped on to the playground. *Come to me, little moth, and catch my flame...* Enzo lifted his lips into a wicked smile. It was time.

He slid behind a large tree on the edge of the playground and waited. He'd been watching Mila for weeks now and kept track of her movements. She had a pattern. Patterns were a person's greatest mistake, and he used them to his advantage. Though, being eight, Mila hadn't learned not to be predictable. All he had to do was remain patient.

As the kids scattered through the playground Mila gravitated toward the lonely tree swing. Not too many kids went to it. They liked to play in groups. Not little Mila. She liked to be alone. Enzo didn't blame her for that. He preferred his own company to anyone else's himself. He stayed hidden until she was near the tree, then stepped behind her as she went for the swing. "Hello, little one," he said softly. His tone was quiet but menacing. "I've been waiting for you."

She turned toward him. Her eyes widened and her mouth fell open. She didn't scream. He expected she might and was prepared to silence her. He wouldn't kill her here. Too messy... Enzo needed complete silence though. "You're a bad man," she said. Her voice was filled with anger. "You killed my father."

Enzo was shocked. How could she possibly know that? Had she seen him in the house? No. He'd been careful. No one was left alive in the house when he left. Enzo was methodical. He didn't make mistakes. "Aren't you a clever little girl." He kneeled so he could meet her gaze. "How did you figure that out?"

She lifted her chin defiantly. "You want to hurt me too."

"Why would I do that?"

"Because you're a bad man. You hurt people."

He couldn't fault her logic. Enzo had never

claimed to be a good man, and he had killed quite a few people. He liked her gumption. It was too bad he did have to kill her...or did he? He never stopped to question why his client wanted the girl dead when it hadn't mattered previously, but Enzo had taken the job, so he'd finish it. Perhaps he'd take the girl and keep her alive for a little while. It might help to taunt the bastard who hounded him to kill her daily. "We've chatted long enough. It's time to leave." He leapt toward her and held a cloth over her mouth until she passed out. Drugs were sloppy, but sometimes he had to use them. He'd take the girl to his hideout, and then he'd make a new plan. One that benefitted him and not the person he worked for. Enzo was tired of taking orders. It was time to build a different life.

PAIGE PACED BACK and forth on the playground. All the children were back inside, and a substitute had been called in to take over her class. She'd called Dane to come pick up Halie. The school wasn't safe. She had thought it would be, and she was wrong. If only she had listened to Lex and Dane. They both had tried to talk her out of going in to work, but she never thought anyone would brazenly abduct a girl from the playground. After school, yes... That's why they were so careful.

Lex came from behind and wrapped his arms around her. "We will find her."

"How can you be so certain." Her entire body shook with rage and anxiety. How dare that man, the evil bastard who killed Mila's parents, take *her* little girl. Mila was part of her family. She had come to mean a lot to her, and she wanted her back. She belonged at home playing with Halie. "You haven't been able to find him. How are we going to get her back when we don't even know who took her?"

"I have an idea," he said. "When you called me, I was at the nursing facility that Mila's grandfather is in. Most days he's incoherent."

"Why does this matter?" Confusion filled her voice. She was tired of worrying, tired of nothing going right, and tired of the lunatic making her life miserable. Paige wanted her girls home, safe and secure. She wanted to fall into bed with Lex and love him all night long. She wanted...peace. Hadn't she suffered enough for one lifetime?

"He was lucid today," Lex explained. "He started screaming early this morning about his son visiting him. The nurses thought he was having a mental break and called in the doctor."

"His son is dead." She scrunched her eyebrows up. "How could he possibly have visited him?"

"His bastard son," Lex said. "No one knew he had another child. Apparently he never talked about him and abandoned him as a boy." He brushed his hand through his dark hair. "He was jealous and killed Antony and Cara Gallo. The bastard came to gloat that he was going to kill all his family members and no one would be left alive. He'd die lost in his own mind with no one to visit him."

"If they had listened to that man earlier, Mila might not have been taken." Anger surged through her, and she wanted to hit something bad. "He would have killed her if he'd found her at the house that day. If she hadn't hidden..."

"Yeah," Lex said solemnly. "She'd be dead."

"What do you do now? How much do you know about this man?"

"His name is Lorenzo Bellanti." Lex sighed. "He has been a hired assassin for years, and is on so many most-wanted lists it's ridiculous. No one has been able to find him. He's good, too good, but I'm still going to find him. I have to."

Paige nodded. "Yes, you do." Mila had to be saved.

She prayed she wasn't asking too much of him. Paige felt responsible for Mila and her current predicament. She wanted to hold the little girl in her arms and reassure herself she was all right. They had to find her. They just had to. "You don't think he's killed her yet, do you?" She had to ask. It was at the forefront of her mind and had been since Mila went missing. "What reason could he have to keep her alive?"

"I don't know," he answered. "I wish I could give you a better answer than that, but it doesn't look good. I want Mila back too, but we have to prepare for the worst. We might not find her alive." His voice was hoarse as he spoke. Tears she'd been holding back started to fall. Lex wrapped his arms around her and held her tight against him. Paige hadn't been this scared in a long time. Not since Nolan. Why did she have to suffer through this agony a second time? Was she being punished.

God, please keep Mila alive...

CHAPTER THIRTEEN

L ex drove Paige to Dane's. She ran to Halie and hugged her tight against her. He didn't blame her. If he had a daughter he'd want to reassure himself she was all right too. A part of him wished he could hug Halie too. He hated that he failed Mila.

"I have to meet Craig," he said to Dane. "I trust you will keep them safe?"

"Always," Dane said. "They're my family." He glanced up at him. "You love her, don't you?"

"Is it that obvious?" He was startled at Dane's observation. Lex barely knew what love was, and he couldn't stop the feeling even if he wanted to. He needed Paige in his life, and he'd fight to keep her in it. The only thing that would keep him from her side was her. If she asked him to leave, he would. Lex would never force her to stay with him. It had to be her choice.

"No," Dane said. "It's not obvious. I know the signs." He gestured across the room to where Reese stood with Paige and Halie. "That woman stole my heart the moment I met her. You look at Paige the way I'm certain I look at my own wife. Only a man in love would notice."

He didn't want to think about Dane's observation. Admitting he was right seemed wrong at the moment. While it might be true, he had other priorities that needed his attention. Later, when he had time to think about everything, he'd re-examine his feelings and Dane's words. Mila needed him to find her, and he prayed he wouldn't be too late when he did.

"I have to go. Call me if..." A lump formed in his throat. He hated that he had to leave Paige and Halie with Dane. "I'll be up most of the night. I don't want to rest until we find Mila."

"Go. They'll be fine here. I promise."

Lex nodded and left. If he didn't go, then he might never leave. He walked slowly to his car, the reluctance to leave heavy in his heart. His phone buzzed as he opened his car door. He slid inside first then answered the call. "We have a lead," Craig said.

"Someone saw a man meeting Bellanti's description at a drugstore earlier today. Apparently he's a regular customer there and picked up a prescription. There's an address, but it's probably false."

"We'll check it out anyway." They had nothing else and had to follow every possibility. "Text me the address and meet me there."

"Will do," Craig answered, then ended the call. Not long after, an address popped up in his text messages. Lex entered it into his GPS and then headed to it. The house was in a remote area with no neighbors. It was actually an ideal place to hide. Could Bellanti have been that careless and used his real address? Why would he do that?

It didn't take him long to reach the house. He parked down the road a bit and then exited the car. He crept toward the house but kept hidden behind a large tree. There were lights on in the main room. The curtains were drawn, but they were nearly transparent. They were probably ancient and threadbare. Lex didn't think anyone had lived in the cabin for a while.

Lex waited. He didn't want to go near the house until Craig arrived. Instead, he stayed to the shadows and watched. A man's voice could be heard, but the words were not so easy to make out. Lex scanned the area and noticed a car, an expensive one, parked in the shadows. The moonlight hit it enough to make out the sheen of silver on the Mercedes-AMG. Lex liked cars, and in a different situation he might drool over that piece of machinery. He narrowed his gaze and attempted to make out the plate, then called in to the station. "I need you to run a plate." He rattled off the information. "It's on a silver Mercedes."

"Got it," the woman on the other end said. "It belongs to one Peter Davis, part owner of Gal-Dav Enterprises, a privately owned company."

Davis...the man who kept calling asking if they had solved the case. How was he involved? Was this his cabin? Did Gal-Dav own it? They did have a real estate division of the company. He'd dig deeper on it. The more evidence they gathered, the stronger their case would be. "Thank you," he said. "That's all I need." He hung up the phone and texted Craig quick. Where the hell was he?

As that thought rolled through his mind he heard the engine of another car. Lex glanced behind him as Craig was exiting his car. He rushed over to Lex's side. "You think this Peter Davis guy is in on it?"

"I think he kept his hands as clean as possible, but yeah, he's dirty." Lex cursed. "He was too interested in what was happening with Mila and if we found the murderer yet."

"We need to get in there."

"Yeah," Lex said. "But we need to be smart about it. Call it in first. We're going to need a team here." They couldn't wait for them to arrive, but at least backup would be on the way. He should have requested it when he called in the plate information. He couldn't make any more mistakes like that. His worry over Mila was making him stupid.

"I'll do it," Craig said. He dialed the station and requested the backup and then nodded at Lex. "What you want to do?"

"You go around back, and I'll take the direct route."

"What?" Craig's voice was high-pitched. "You're going to brazenly walk to the front door and do what? Kindly ask for them to return the little girl and think they'll comply?"

"No, well, partly." Lex sighed. "Davis contacts me. He knows I have contact with Mila. He won't expect you to be around, but me, he'll expect. You're my ace. I need you to have my back on this. Can I count on you?"

"You know you can," Craig said. "All right." He

blew out a breath. "Give me five minutes before you make your move."

Lex nodded. "Go."

Craig sprinted to the back of the cabin. Lex waited the allotted time then meandered to the front door and knocked. Brazen? He wasn't usually, but he'd put his life on the line to save Mila. He prayed he wasn't too late. The voices inside were muffled and stopped as soon as he knocked. The door swung open and Peter Davis was on the other side. "Detective Foster," he said with surprise in his tone. "How did you know to find me here?"

"May I come in?" he asked. "I have information on Mila Gallo, and I know you'll be interested."

He glanced behind him first. Then said, "Of course, come on in."

Lex stepped into the cabin. He kept his attention on his surroundings. There had been another man in the cabin talking to Peter Davis. Where had he gone, and was it Lorenzo Bellanti? He turned toward Peter and said, "I'm not certain if you've heard. Mila Gallo was taken from school today."

"She was?" he said. Peter acted surprised, but Lex wasn't buying it. "Who took her?"

"We're not certain," he answered. "No one saw

anything. I know how concerned you have been for her welfare. I thought you might want to help."

"Yes, I would. What can I do to assist you?" He held his hand over his heart. Lex refrained, barely, from rolling his eyes. "Mila is like a daughter to me. I want to do anything I can."

The man oozed fake charm. He was as slimy as a frog swimming in a moss covered pond. Lex would bet he was knee deep in the muck too. "We are at a dead end on the case. None of our leads have panned out. Is there anything you can think of? Why would someone want to murder the Gallos and kidnap their daughter?"

He was waiting for Craig. Was he inside the house? Where was the other man that had been talking to Peter? Nothing seemed to be going quite how he'd envisioned it. He glanced around the room. There was no signs anyone else had been in there. He had a feeling this wasn't where Peter stayed though. The man hadn't come out and said it, but he'd caught him off guard. Why hadn't he asked again how Lex had found him? He dropped his inquiry rather fast when he said he had information about Mila.

"No," he said. "I'm afraid I have no idea why

anyone would want to hurt them. They are or were wonderful people."

There was a bit of noise in the back of the house. Like something was scuffling or scooting against a wall or floor. "What was that?"

"It's nothing," Peter waved his hand. "Probably the dog. I can go check on it."

Lex didn't wait for him to do any such thing. It gave him probable cause to investigate. Dog? He doubted that very much. Craig could be in trouble. He rushed toward where the sounds had come from. When he entered the room, he found Craig struggling with a man. He had dark hair tied back in a ponytail. Craig got a good punch in and the man fell backward.

"What the hell?" Peter Davis said. "What's going on here?"

"Don't act innocent," the other man said. His accent thick, as he spoke.

"You should have stayed hidden, Enzo," Peter said. Disapproval reverberated through his tone. "Now there's no going back."

Lex glanced from Peter to Enzo. This was not going to end well. He had to act fast before something terrible happened. Mila was his first priority, but he also didn't want either perp to get free either.

They had to pay for their crimes. They both had a lot to answer for, starting with the Gallo's murder. He had a feeling they had done more than that though.

"It was already too late. Your incompetence led to this. This is *your* fault. You insisted the brat had to be dealt with. Your greediness is your undoing." He lunged toward Peter, but he didn't reach him. Peter pulled out a gun and shot him in the head, then aimed at Craig and pulled the trigger. Lex had pulled his gun out when shots were fired. Craig jerked back and fell to the ground. He might still be alive, and Lex prayed he was. "He outran his usefulness." Peter turned to Lex. He seemed pretty calm about the whole thing, and that unnerved Lex a little. He kept his gun aimed at Peter. He had to stop him before he hurt anyone else. "This is all messier than it needed to be. When the authorities arrive, they'll find you all...dead. It's unfortunate, but I must erase his mistakes. If he'd killed the girl weeks ago, this wouldn't have happened."

"Where's Mila?" He kept his attention focused on Peter. "What have you done with her?" He moved slowly toward him. Every little inch helped to close that distance. Then he would have a better chance of taking him down.

"I did nothing," he said. His voice was eerily calm.

"Enzo took her and drugged her. She's asleep in the other room still. Not for long though. She'll die after you. It has to happen if I'm to claim Antony's half of the company. With her alive, she inherits. I cannot allow that to happen." He raised his gun higher. "Are you ready to die, detective?"

"Not today," he said and fired before Peter could. The man fell hard, but it hadn't been a kill shot. He was still breathing and could shoot. Lex rushed to his side and punched him and stepped on his wrist. He kicked the gun out of his reach then handcuffed him quick, then checked for more weapons, and breathed a sigh of relief when he didn't find any. The last thing he needed was a surprise attack from the bastard. Backup should arrive soon, and he had to get to Mila. He took a tissue out of a nearby box and picked up the gun to keep it out of Peter's reach. With it secure, he could search for Mila. He needed to check on Craig, but Mila was a little girl, and his instincts were driving him to guarantee her safety above all. Lex prayed Craig was alive, and he'd ensure help came to keep him that way after he located Mila.

. . .

HE RAN to the other room and found her on a bed. Her hands were tied to the headboard. Lex quickly undid the rope and carried her out of the room. He took her to his car and placed her in the backseat. She'd be safe there while he checked on Craig. Mila would have to go to the hospital to be checked on later too.

With Mila safe, he could take care of everything else. He rushed inside and went to Craig's side. He checked for a pulse and breathed a sigh of relief. He was alive. Lex plucked his phone out of his pocket and called for an ambulance. "I have three GSW victims. Send a bus immediately. One dead, two still alive." He rattled off the information and ended the call. Craig's eyelids fluttered open. "How are you feeling?"

"Like I've been shot," he groaned out the words. "Did we get them?"

"Yeah, we did," Lex said. "Relax. Help is on the way."

"I'll close my eyes for a little while. Wake me when it's over."

As Craig's eyelids shut, several officers rushed inside. It was chaotic for several moments. Lex answered all their questions and stayed until Craig was loaded into an ambulance and Peter Davis was placed in a different one. He'd have to be treated before he could be locked in a cell. When he got back to his car, Mila was starting to wake up. He opened his car door and said, "Hello, sprite, how are you feeling?"

"Lex?" she croaked out his name.

"Yes, it's me," he reassured her. "Lay down and rest." He wanted to hold her tight and reassure himself she hadn't been hurt. He adored her and wanted to keep her safe always.

He called Paige and told her he'd found Mila and told her to meet him at the hospital. She was waiting in the emergency room when he walked in with the little girl. She took her from him and held her tight. His heart beat heavily in his chest, but it warmed a little at the sight of Paige holding Mila. His girls were safe. He could breathe easier.

"You're squeezing me," Mila said.

"I'm sorry," Paige said. "I was so scared."

"Me too," Mila whispered. "But I knew Lex would save me."

"Of course he did," Paige said. She glanced at him as she continued to hug Mila tight. "We can always count on him. I'm going to let the doctors examine you now." A nurse took Mila from her and carried her into an examine room. Paige kept her gaze trained on them until they disappeared from sight. Once she was reassured Mila was safe, Paige came back to him and hugged him. "Thank you."

"You don't need to thank me for doing my job." He pulled her close. "I'd do anything for you and the girls. I love you."

"I love you too," she said as she stepped out of his arms, but remained close. "I didn't think I was capable of giving my heart to anyone. I don't know how much you've heard about my past..." She cleared her throat. "About Halie's father..."

"You don't need to tell me this," he told her. Lex didn't want her to open wounds she'd buried. He knew enough to realize Nolan Pratt had put her through hell.

"I do," she insisted. Paige rubbed her hands over her arms nervously, then met his gaze. "Nolan broke something inside of me. I thought I'd never move past it, and wanted to find a way to redeem myself. It wasn't until this moment that I realized I don't need redemption. What he did...that was wrong. I thought I had failed Halie and myself. It's time I forgave myself for that and accept I have a right to happiness. This needs to be said now. It needs to be clear so there's no doubt what I want and hope for: I want you to be a part of my life." She took a deep breath "That is, if you want to be."

How could he not love this woman? To him, she wasn't broken. She was the strongest woman he'd ever known. He couldn't imagine not having her in his life. She made him want more, and he hoped, in time, they would have everything together. He'd wait forever for her if she asked him to. Thankfully she wasn't though.

"Of course I do," he said. "How could I not? I didn't believe in love until you." He brushed a stray lock of her hair behind her ear. "I've been thinking about what I want in my life. It begins and ends with you. I can't lose you. I don't want to live without you. The very idea of not waking up next to you guts me. I'd be a fool to walk away from the best thing in my life. I'm yours as long as you'll have me. There's not enough time in the world to satisfy my need to be with you."

"Good," she said. "Because I'm thinking forever isn't nearly long enough." She walked back into his arms and rested her head on his shoulder. She glanced up at him. "Let's finish here and take Mila home, we can pick up Halie on the way. I don't want to waste any time starting our life together."

It had been a long few weeks. He hoped they

were done with the unnecessary excitement for a while. Lex wanted to love Paige and bask in some peace and quiet for a little while. The bad guys were caught, and Mila was safe. Paige loved him. In fifty years, he'd look back on this moment as the beginning of his happy ending. He had love and family. There was nothing else he could possibly want. All was right in his world...

EPILOGUE

Ten years later...

Mila stared out the window of her bedroom. It was her birthday. Halie and she had graduated high school a couple months ago and soon they would both be going to college. Halie wanted to be a lawyer. She'd been interning with Matthew Price, a friend of their parents. Mila wanted to be a therapist, one as good as Dr. Adams. She wanted to help people, in a similar way that she'd been as a little girl.

Paige and Lex had married a year after she'd come to live with them, and they adopted her soon after. They loved her as if she were their own. She couldn't have asked for a more loving home.

Her biological parents had loved her. She didn't doubt that for a moment, and if they had not been murdered, they would have given her a good life. It would have been different, but still wonderful. Aside from that tragedy, her life with her first family had been unremarkable. Her father had been, not cold exactly, but formal. He'd had expectations and would get angry if they were not met. So Mila had done her best not to experience his temper. He had never been *Daddy* to her. Always *Father*...

Lex became her daddy. He'd protected her and loved her as if she was his daughter, and then when he adopted her he became her dad in truth. Nothing had prepared her for how much that would mean to her. She became Mila Foster that day and left Mila Gallo behind her. She never wanted to be that girl ever again. It was her new chance at life, and she'd embraced it from that moment on.

"Mila," Halie called out, "come on, we're going to be late."

Mila grinned. Halie was always so impatient. They had plans to meet friends at Snowberry for ice cream. Mila glanced at her bed. Elsa Two sat on the pillow. She still slept with the polar bear and suspected she would forever. It comforted her when she was at her worst. Paige had apologized over and over that the first Elsa had been destroyed. She had never said how, but Mila knew. She'd requested her parents's police file when she was fifteen. At the time, she had to know all the details. What had happened to the first bear was included along with pictures. She'd never told Paige she'd seen the remnants of her bear. Mila was glad she hadn't witnessed its destruction the day it had happened. That might have been too much trauma for her fragile mind.

"I'll be down in a minute," Mila yelled. She needed a few more moments. Some days it was hard to believe that it had been almost ten years since her parents were murdered. She picked up her polar bear and hugged him close. Mila needed the comfort before she went to get ice cream with her friends. Somehow it seemed right. She mourned the loss of her mother and father and what they could have had as a family. While she had been fortunate, she still felt their loss every day.

A knock echoed through the room. "Mila?" Paige said. She stopped suddenly and asked, "Are you all right?"

"I'm fine," she told her. "Just feeling a little sentimental."

Paige crossed the room and hugged her. Mila

stopped calling Paige and Lex by their first name years ago, but sometimes, like today, it was harder to refer to them as *Mom* and *Dad* in her mind. It almost felt like she was betraying her parents.

"It's your birthday," Paige reassured her. "It's all right to miss them."

How did she do that? She always seemed to know what to say or what Mila might be thinking. "Is it?"

"Of course it is." Paige stepped back and then cupped her cheek. "They're your parents, and you lost them in one of the worst possible ways. You're about to take a huge step in your life. With so many changes on the horizon, it's normal to reflect on your past."

Mila supposed that was true, but she hated it all the same. Maybe she should make an appointment with Dr. Adams. She still had sessions with her every now and then when she felt she needed them. It didn't happen as much as it had in the early days. Speaking with Dr. Adams reinforced all the progress she'd made over the years.

"I suppose that is true." She smiled. "Thank you."

"For what?" Paige asked.

"For being there for me and helping me through everything."

Paige's lips wobbled a little as if she were fighting tears. She touched the corner of her eyes briefly. "It's been my pleasure having you here. I should be the one thanking you. Now, come on downstairs. Lex has a surprise for you before you go celebrate with your friends."

Mila smiled. "Should I be scared?" Lex was warm and serious at the same time. He was always concerned about her and Halie's safety. She hoped this wasn't another bright idea for self-defense lessons. Though, she had to admit, those might come in handy, and the classes had been fun.

"I don't believe so." She grinned. His surprise could be anything. "But you never do know with Lex."

Mila set her polar bear down and followed Paige out of her room. They went down the stairs and found Lex in the living room with his arm crossed. "It's about time. I was starting to think you were sprouting roots upstairs."

"I didn't know there was any reason to rush." She closed the distance between them and hugged Lex. "What do you need me for?" Mila kept her tone light and cheerful as she spoke.

Lex wrapped his arms around her. "I don't know.

This seems like a good enough reason to have you come downstairs." She loved Lex's hugs. They always made her feel safe and loved.

She giggled and then stepped out of his arms. "That's not why you wanted to see me, and you know it." Mila crossed her arms over her chest. "Where's my surprise."

"In good time, my child," he said in a teasing tone. "Come outside."

They walked to the kitchen and into the back-yard. It was decorated with streamers, balloons, and a large trampoline filled with little bouncy balls along the netted sides. All her family was there too. Halie, Dane, Reese, and even Dr. Adams stood near a table filled with gifts. They started singing "Happy Birthday" when she stepped out on to the porch. A cake sat on a table nearby in the shape of a polar bear with two candles on it, one and eight, lit and ready for her to blow the flames out.

"Happy birthday, darling," Paige said. Her voice cracked as she spoke.

Lex pulled her close and said in a husky tone. "Here's to many more to come." He almost looked close to tears too.

"I love you both so much," she said, her voice hoarse with emotion. Tears fell down her cheeks.

This was what happiness felt like. She may have had a lot of loss, but she had also gained so much out of it. Perhaps it was past time she accepted that and continued to move forward. Only good things and happy thoughts for her future.

Thank you so much for taking the time to read my book.

Your opinion matters!

Please take a moment to review this book on your favorite review site and share your opinion with fellow readers.

www.authordawnbrower.com

EXCERPT: ONE HEART TO GIVE

HEART'S INTENT BOOK ONE

ONE HEART
TO GIVE

USA TODAY BESTSELLING AUTHOR
DAWN BROWER

ONE HEART TO GIVE

When tragedy strikes Dani's business partner it brings Ren back into her life. She'd thought she moved past her feelings for him, but one glance and they come flooding back.

Growing up as an orphan, Daniella Brosen has trouble connecting with other people. She has no room for anyone in her life, except her best friend, Rendall Sousa. He is the only male she's ever loved or will love. Circumstances beyond her control tear them apart, and she has no choice but to leave him behind.

When Daniella left without a word it broke Ren's heart. If she'd given him a chance he'd have told her how much he loved her. Dani was everything to him, but she made her choice. There was only one course of action left to him—move on without her.

As their lives become intertwined again, can Ren convince her he's always loved her or will she push him away forever?

PROLOGUE

Ten years earlier

Daniella spun around in her prom dress. The dark green gown shimmered in the sunlight streaming through her bedroom window. She didn't have a date. It should bother her, but it didn't. There was one boy she wanted to go with: her best friend, Rendell Sousa. Ren was so handsome, strong, and perfect in every way. The only downside was he had a girlfriend. She hated Jessica Clarke. The girl owned a part of him Dani never would.

She'd planned on skipping prom, but Ren had talked her into going. He said he could have two dates. It would have been easier to say no... He made it impossible to turn him down, stating he couldn't go to prom without both his girls. Jessica wouldn't be happy at the idea of sharing Ren, and Dani didn't want to upset her by going along with his plan. She told him no until he agreed to arrange for a group of friends to join them. Even with that idea, Dani decline anyway. Ren was insistent and too persuasive for her to resist. Not having a dress wouldn't even be a deterrent.

He'd talked Sarah, another friend of theirs, into taking her shopping. Dani had dipped into her savings, using the money meant for college to pay for it. Her foster family didn't help her with anything they didn't deem necessary. A prom dress was not high on that list, like most things Dani may want or even need. It was why she worked after school most days.

Now she stood in front of her bedroom mirror, admiring the green satin dress. It was worth it. The dress was amazing and it made her feel like a fairy-tale princess. She glanced at the clock and hurried to finish the last minute preparations. Ren would be by to pick her up at any moment.

"Dani," her foster mother yelled. "Ren is here."

"Time to face the music." She ran her hands over her dress to ease her nerves. Would he like what he saw? It wouldn't matter. She couldn't let it because

Ren had a girlfriend. She started down the stairs and stopped at the bottom. Ren looked gorgeous in his tux. He'd opted for a white jacket with a black tie. It wasn't the usual black penguin suit almost every other boy would no doubt choose to wear. He looked amazing and absolutely gorgeous. His rich golden brown hair was brushed back and his wicked grin made him even more devastating.

"Are you ready?" he asked. "Jessica's already in the car."

She nodded and let him lead her out the door. This was foolish. Dani hated being the third wheel on his date. It didn't matter that a group of friends were going together. She would end up between Ren and Jessica in some way. He wouldn't allow her to essentially be a wallflower. He had always been protective of her. She should have said no. It would have been better for them both if she had. Why had she let him talk her into this? Jessica would do something to make her miserable. Ren didn't see her the way Dani did. Her viperous tongue only came out when Ren wasn't around to hear it. Jessica made sure they were in private when her worst came out to play.

"Are you excited?" Stupid question. Why would he be?

"I'm looking forward to dancing with you later." He smiled softly. "And with Jessica too."

Dani frowned. Why did he feel the need to add that part in? Of course he would look forward to dancing with his girlfriend. He didn't need to remind her of that. Tiny pinpricks of pain shot through her heart. She couldn't let him know how much it hurt her to see him with Jessica. He deserved to be happy. She chose this path. He was her best friend, and she wanted him to be happy. She'd smile and fake it as long as she could. Ren didn't need to know she'd fallen in love with him. The burden was hers and hers alone.

He opened the door to the limo. She peeked inside and let out a relieved breath. A group of their friends were already inside. Most of them were also dateless. At least she didn't have to suffer in awkward silence while they picked everyone up. Ren must have saved her for last. She waved at them and hopped in. She sat across from Ren and Jessica next to another male friend of theirs. It didn't take long for the car to get to their destination. Prom was being held at the Tempest Ballroom on the opposite side of town. It was where it was always held. Ren was the first out of the limo and helping all the girls out.

"I forgot to tell you how pretty you look," he said as he held his hand out to her. "You're going to break some hearts in there."

She laughed. "I doubt it."

His gaze seemed to go unfocused for a second before he shook his head. Something bothered him; whatever it was he was holding it inside. "Trust me on this."

She wouldn't push. The night was supposed to be fun. If he wanted to tell her he would. For now, they would go inside and enjoy the evening. "If you say so." She shrugged. "I'm not holding my breath."

"Can we go inside now?" Jessica whined. "You're supposed to be my date." She glared at Dani, letting her gaze roll over her as if she'd witnessed something disgusting.

Ren turned to her and pulled her into his arms. He placed a quick kiss on her lips. "And that I am. Let's go see what the fuss is all about." He held out his arm to Dani. "You coming?"

She shook her head. "Give me a minute. I'll be in later. Take Jessica inside."

He frowned. "Are you sure?"

She didn't want to explain that she needed time to build up her strength. It would take all she had to get through the evening of their lovey dovey affection. She couldn't stand Jessica, and that wasn't only because the other girl had something she wanted. Jessica was mean and spiteful. For the life of her, Dani couldn't figure out what Ren saw in her.

"Go." She pushed at him. "I'll be fine. Promise."

He stared at her for a few seconds and then nodded in agreement. Dani breathed a sigh of relief as she watched them go.

"Why aren't you going inside?" Brian asked. He was one of the friends who'd traveled with them in the limo. "Something preventing you from entering? Did Cinderella already lose her shoe?"

"Ha. Ha," Dani mocked. "I'm far from the unwanted stepsister." No she was plain unwanted. Her mother had tossed her aside when she was a little girl, left her on a church doorstep for someone to find. She'd never know who her real parents were. They probably had been teenagers with no ability to care for her.

"Why don't you push her out of the way and claim your prince," Brian asked. "You know you want to."

She scrunched up her nose and winced. "Ren is not my prince." He never would be.

"Maybe not. But don't you think it's time to

admit that there's more than friendship between the two of you?"

Was Brian drunk? There was, and always would be, nothing but friendship between her and Ren. She was all right with that. Honestly she was. *Yeah, keep saying that Dani, maybe one day you will convince yourself it's true.* She loved him. Unfortunately, he loved Jessica. Maybe it was time she put some distance between her and Ren. Being around him hurt too damn much, and she wasn't strong enough to handle it. Graduation loomed on the horizon. She'd make a break for it and not look back.

"Deny it all you want. It's not my place to convince you. Come on, let's go inside."

Nothing would persuade her. Ren loved Jessica. Dani wouldn't get between them. She followed Brian inside and steeled herself to pretend to be happy.

REN WATCHED for her to enter. He didn't know why she refused to come inside with him and Jessica, but he worried. If she didn't show up soon he'd go look for her. The dress she'd chosen was sinful on her perfect body. The shimmering green matched her eyes, and her dark midnight tresses fell down her shoulder in curls. He wanted to run his hands through her hair and feel the silky softness. Why couldn't he feel that way about Jessica? She was nice enough, and lovely to look at. He'd started dating her to try to take his mind off the one he wanted, his best friend. Dani had said over and over how much she appreciated him. She was glad they were friends and she could rely on him—how lost she'd be without their friendship. It grated on his nerves every time those words came out of her mouth. Didn't she see how much he wanted her? Dani owned his heart. If only she wanted to be more than friends...

But she didn't, and why not date Jessica? At least she saw him as boyfriend material. Sometimes he regretted that choice. All right, most days he did, and he'd almost broken up with her several times. Then Dani would repeat her friendship tirade. Nothing pissed him off more and made him dig his feet in with innate stubbornness than listening to that. He shouldn't let it bother him, but he couldn't help what he felt. In truth, he wasn't doing himself, Jessica, or Dani any favors by denying them. Both girls deserved better, and soon he'd own up to everything. When the time was right he'd break up with Jessica and be honest with Dani. Prom night wasn't the night for shattering hearts and confessions.

Ren frowned as she walked in with Brian. Were they seeing each other? He'd thought they were friends, but he could be wrong. Jealousy welled up inside of him. He clenched his fists at his side. He would not make a scene. If Brian was the one Dani wanted, he wouldn't get in her way. He had a girl-friend, and he shouldn't be mooning over his best friend. She would be the first to tell him that.

"Come on, let's dance." Jessica pulled him toward the dance floor.

He allowed it and did the best he could to pretend Dani wasn't staring at another boy. He wanted her, always had. It hurt to watch her with someone else, especially since she'd never seemed interested in someone else. She didn't date, said it was a waste of her time. She had plans and a boyfriend would deter them. Dani worked hard at everything so she could leave their small town behind and never look back. Had she changed her mind? Did she consider dating an option now? Maybe he could finally convince her they should be more than friends. He gulped back the lump in his throat and glanced down at Jessica. She seemed so happy and carefree. The strands of music ended and everyone broke apart. Ren didn't want to dance any longer. He had to find Dani. It was an impulse he couldn't resist. She was on the other side of the room laughing with Brian. He headed toward them, Jessica close behind.

"I see you made it inside," he said.

Dani smiled. "Did you think I'd get lost?"

He pasted a happy expression on his face. She didn't need to know he'd worried. "Of course not."

"They have some awful punch and snacks set out." Brian gestured toward a table nearby. "I damn near spit the crap out. I barely managed to swallow it, and choked it down. Dani thought it was hilarious."

"Oh, come on." She laughed again. "It couldn't be that bad."

Ren gritted his teeth together. He had to do something to stop this...whatever it was between Brian and Dani. He couldn't take it. It was time to stop fooling himself. He wanted to step back and let her be happy with someone else, but in reality it was impossible. The strands of a slow song started to fill his ears. He held his hand out to his best friend. "Come dance with me."

She nodded and placed her hand in his. "Oh yes, please, I love this song."

He didn't stop to look at anyone. His gaze was locked firmly on Dani's face. He didn't care if Brian was mad he'd usurped his time with her. Jessica knew Dani was his best friend. This wasn't the first time they'd danced, and she'd understand. Well, as much as any girl would he supposed. Ren couldn't make himself care. This was what he wanted and the rest of them be damned. He glanced across the room and noticed there were a lot of people dancing with someone they'd not arrived with. It was perfectly normal for him to enjoy a dance with someone other than Jessica. It was high school and prom was supposed to be fun—a memory they'd keep forever.

Let me love you... He wanted to say that to her. The song wasn't a perfect fit. But he wanted to say some of those very words to her. She deserved to be cherished. They swayed to the music. She glanced up at him and stole his breath. For a moment, he could pretend they were together and had a future together. He wanted to give her everything, show her the way love was supposed to be. He wanted to hold her as more than a friend.

The music ended and they stood there, staring at each other. Everything else ceased to exist. It was just the two of them locked in beautiful moment he wanted to burn in his memory. Her full sultry lips tilted into a brilliant smile, and her gaze radiated happiness. It left him with a warm and fuzzy glow spreading through his whole body. Until the spell was broken by his actual girlfriend—Jessica always did have the worst timing.

"It's my turn," Jessica demanded and pushed Dani aside.

For a brief moment, everything had been so perfect. The smile on Dani's face fell before she turned to head off the dance floor. He reached for her, but Jessica demanded his attention. Dani was all the way across the room before he could do anything to stop her. The dance had been worth every second of the clinginess he was about to endure from his girlfriend. She said she understood his friendship with Dani, but if he paid any amount of attention to her, Jessica ultimately became jealous.

He understood it, even as it irritated him. He couldn't blame her. They were dating, but he wouldn't stop being Dani's friend, even if it tore at him in every possible way. Ren glanced across the room and located Dani. He couldn't go after her to see what was wrong, at least not yet. He would later when he could shake Jessica for a few minutes.

"Finally," Jessica complained. "I thought that song

would never end. I don't know why you feel as if you need to placate her."

Ren clenched his hand into a fist at his side and reminded himself Jessica didn't understand. She didn't realize he loved Dani in a way he could never love her. It was time to break up with her. Not at the dance, but definitely before graduation in a couple weeks. He'd tell Dani how much he loved her. It was time to man up and own his feelings.

DANI PUSHED her way into the girl's restroom and sighed in relief when she found it empty. She needed a breather from the hot dance floor and Jessica's glaring eyes. Every time she looked over at Ren, she would meet Jessica's gaze. The girl had every right to hate her. Ren tended to drop everything if Dani needed him for any reason. That's what friends did for each other. Dani didn't want to make him stop either, and yes, she depended on him. He was the only one she let get even remotely close to her.

She loved him.

The dance had been perfect. For a small moment in time she could pretend they were more than friends. That she allowed him to be hers in every way she wanted him to be. It had all come to a screeching halt when Jessica stormed over to them at the end. The spell had been broken and she had to go back to being his best friend.

Dani headed over to the sink, turned it on, allowing the cool water to run over her fingers. She splashed a little on her heated cheeks. It felt amazing washing over her warm skin. She turned the water off, grabbed a paper towel to dry her hands, and then tossed it in a nearby trash can. It was time to go back to the dance and pretend everything was all right.

"I saw you come in here, and I think it's time you and I have a little talk."

Dani spun around and met Jessica's gaze. She wanted to groan, but repressed it. At some point she should have known Jessica would confront her. She always did. Ren's girlfriend would spout out her demands to leave him alone and then drive home the final point—*she* was his girlfriend, not Dani. As if Dani needed the reminder. Maybe she did on some level. She hated sharing him. It grated on her in so many ways. She made her choices though, and now had the pleasure of living with them. Dani grimaced as she swallowed down that bitter pill. Pleasure? It was far from it.

"I think you've said everything you need to say to me." Dani turned away from her. "You say it so often I could repeat it verbatim."

"No. I haven't said all there is to say." Jessica pushed Dani's shoulder. "Look at me."

Dani rolled her eyes and turned back to Jessica. What did she want now? Did she really feel the need to mark her territory again? And yeah, in Jessica's mind Ren was hers to mark. He couldn't be friends with Dani while he dated her. Yes, Dani loved him, but she never made a move on him. She kept things strictly platonic. That was the whole meaning of friendship after all. Anything else would muddy the waters, and she could lose what little she did have with him forever. It was why she insisted at the beginning they be just friends. Friendships lasted far longer than any other relationship.

"What do you want?" Dani folded her arms across her chest. "I would like to get back to the dance."

"Why?" She raised an eyebrow. "So you can insinuate yourself further into Ren's life?"

She wasn't having this argument with Jessica. "I don't know how many times I have to tell you that Ren and I are *friends*." She glared at her. The more Jessica said the more pissed off she was becoming.

She got it. Honestly she did, but she was sick of listening to it. Nothing she said to Jessica would make her feel better. "There is nothing other than that going on between us."

"I have eyes, you know." Jessica took a step closer. "I can see how you look at him. I know you want to be more than friends. I'm not going to stand here and let you come between us. I'm done with you and your neediness."

"I don't know what to tell you." Dani sighed and shook her head. "I'm not going to stop being Ren's friend to make you feel secure in your relationship." She couldn't imagine a life without Ren in it. He was the one person she could always depend on when everything seemed to be falling apart. Every one needed at least one person they could rely on. For Dani, it had always been Ren.

"Do you even know how he really feels about you?" Jessica sneered and took a step closer to Dani. There was barely any room between them as she angrily retorted, "Because let me tell you, he's not as happy as he seems when having to constantly run whenever you need him."

She was lying. Ren wouldn't talk badly about her. Would he? He always seemed happy to help her. He was the one who'd talked her into going to prom. It was his idea for them all to come together. Jessica was pissed because Ren danced with her. That was all this was about, and she wouldn't let her get to her. "Ren is a big boy. He can make decisions for himself. He doesn't need you to fight his battles for him." If he was annoyed with Dani for any reason, he'd tell her himself. It'd never stopped him in the past. Ren was the most vocal person she knew.

Jessica lifted her hands and pushed Dani hard, taking her by surprise. Pain shot through her backside as it met the floor with a hard thump. She wanted to jump to her feet and punch Jessica's perfect face, but it wouldn't do any good. The girl wanted to fight. Dani wouldn't humor her. Ren would be in the middle of it all, and Dani wanted to do what was best for her friend. Fighting with his girlfriend wasn't going to make things easier on any of them. She took a deep breath and prepared to reason with the girl. "Go back to the dance." Dani said calmly. "I don't want to do this with you."

"Too bad. It's time we settled things once and for all. I'm tired of you getting in the middle of my relationship. School is almost over, and Ren and I have plans. They don't include you."

Dani knew what Ren's plans were. Where he was going to college, what medical school he hoped to get into, and his need to help others. Jessica should know he would share that with her. "I don't have time for your histrionics." Dani got to her feet and brushed down her skirt. "I won't mention any of this to Ren." She walked past Jessica and headed to the exit.

"Not so fast." Jessica grabbed her arm preventing her from leaving. "I'm not done. You don't leave until I have my say."

She gritted her teeth together. Jessica was so damn demanding. Dani couldn't believe she called her the needy one. The girl insisted on getting her way far too often. This was the last time she gave in and conceded. "You always have something you have to say. What is it this time?" Dani raised an eyebrow mockingly. "Ren actually hates me? He only puts up with me out of a habit? I've heard it all from you. What makes this any different?"

Jessica raised her hand and slapped her. The sting spread across her cheek in tiny pinpricks. Dani rubbed her hand over her face and glared at the other girl. "I'm done with you. Don't corner me again. If you leave me alone, I'll do the same."

"No. I'm not going to step aside and let you ruin my relationship with him. I'm tired of him always running to do something for you. Find your own boyfriend. Ren is mine."

Dani stepped close to Jessica and stared into her eyes. "Ren is my friend. Get used to it. I will always be a part of his life." Even when it hurt too much to be around him… It was the path she chose. "Now I'm going to go back to the dance and try to enjoy what's left of it. I'll do you a solid and not mention this to Ren because I'm not the vindictive bitch you seem to think I am."

Dani turned to leave once again but stopped short when she heard Jessica say, "I'm pregnant."

Dani closed her eyes as her words washed over her. They froze her heart. Any hope she'd thought she had with Ren evaporated. He would never abandon Jessica and his child. She turned toward Jessica. Tears were falling down her cheeks. She was fighting to hold onto Ren. It didn't matter how Dani felt about the girl. She was going to have Ren's baby. There was only one decision she could make.

"Does Ren know?"

She shook her head. "I haven't told him yet."

"Why are you telling me?" She should be having this conversation with Ren. "You should tell him." What game was Jessica playing? There had to be a reason she was dropping this particular bomb on Dani.

"I want you to leave us alone. We don't stand a chance with you constantly around us. We deserve to have the best possible start. Our child needs both parents to be completely devoted to it."

She was right. Dani knew it. She was done fighting fate. Ren couldn't even be her friend anymore. He wouldn't be solely focused on his family if he was always hanging around with her. If she needed him, he'd come running. For his sake, and his child's, she would have to disappear and allow him the chance to be happy.

She nodded. "You win. You have until graduation to tell Ren. If you don't, I will." Dani turned and left the room. The roles had reversed, and now she was the one fighting tears. She'd lost something significant to her, and there wasn't a damn thing she could do about it. She left the dance and walked the entire way home. It gave her time to work out what had to be done. There wasn't much of a choice left. She had to leave, and the sooner the better.

REN NEVER GOT the chance to tell Dani he loved her. She ran away before graduation. He'd been blindsided by her choice, and beyond pissed off. What had he ever done to her to deserve such little regard? He searched for her. She'd hidden herself too well. If she really didn't want him in her life any longer, he'd respect her wishes. Ren always did what Dani wanted. Probably always would. They'd set that pattern up early on in their relationship. "Friends forever," she'd said. How wrong she'd been; how pitiful he was. He'd been a fool to believe they could have anything…

"Damn you, Dani," he shouted. Tears fell from his eyes. How was he supposed to let her go? She'd been a part of his life for as long as he could remember. Now he was alone. A piece of him would always be missing without her in his life. What if he never loved again? He doubted he truly could. He only had one heart to give—and Dani owned it. She left him with a hole in his chest and nothing to fill the void.

Jessica had become more attentive. He'd allowed her to somewhat fill what was missing, even though a part of him screamed in protest. What else was he to do? There wasn't much choice left to him. Dani had taken all of them away. He wanted to hate her for it, and maybe he even did on a small level. One day maybe they would see each other again, and he'd be able to ask her why. Until then he was left with so many questions, and absolutely no answers.

He always came back to one thing. Why. Why had she left? He should have known something was wrong. She'd been so weird at prom—after they danced. He'd meant to ask her what was bothering her, but she'd disappeared before it ended. Brian had been no help, when he'd asked him about Dani. No one had seen her or noticed when she'd left. The next day she'd been gone. All her foster parents were able to tell him was she had decided to leave for college early.

So much for confessing he'd love her forever.

He was a damned idiot. The biggest and most moronic fool alive—how could he have believed he could have it all? Some things were not meant to be. Sadly he couldn't do anything to change the feelings rolling through his heart. He'd always love her, nothing, and no one would ever change that. His heart would be hers, and anyone else who came into his life wouldn't compare.

No, this couldn't be the end. He wouldn't accept that. Someday, he promised himself, if he found Dani again he'd make sure she stayed around long enough to realize what she meant to him. What they'd lost by her actions. It was the only thing he could hold onto. When he saw her again, and he fully believed he would, there would be nothing to stand in his way—even Dani herself.

"One day, Dani, love." He stared up at the sky. "I will find you, and if we're both lucky enough we will find a way to be together." Ren rubbed his chest trying to erase the ache that filled his heart. "Nothing will be the same until that day, but I promise we can make it right if we fight hard enough."

She was worth fighting for. The best things in life were. It might just take longer than he'd like to make his promise a reality. As time went by, he'd do everything in his power to hold on to hope. It was the only thing he had left. If he lost it, then all would be lost. There would never be a Dani and Ren. There would be nothingness.

"I'll do my best," he whispered. "But I'm far from perfect."

And there was Jessica. She wanted more than he'd been willing to give. It was a temptation he was finding harder and harder to resist. In time he was afraid he'd give in. Life had a funny way of throwing a wrench in even the best laid plans. There was no telling what his future had in store for him, but he had hopes, dreams, and wishes he hoped to one day see fulfilled. Dani was one part of that bigger picture. If he couldn't have her, at least he could have the rest. He'd work hard and achieve what he could. Maybe, somewhere along the way, he'd discover that he could live without her.

He snorted. "Not likely."

But he'd attempt to. Oh he'd try; he had no choice after all.

CHAPTER ONE

"Excuse me, Ms. Brosen," Claire said as she knocked on the door. "You have a call on line one. It sounds important."

Dani sighed and set down the motion she was reading over. She didn't have time for interruptions. Her partner, Matthew Price, had been a no-show at the office. The case they were working on was both high profile and potentially career making. It could make or break their practice. He knew how important the motion was. He was late. It both irritated and worried her. Matt was usually reliable.

She lifted the receiver and placed it against her ear, and then pressed the button for line one. "Daniella Brosen, how can I help you?"

"This is Lana Kelly. I'm calling from Envill East."

"Yes?" Why was someone from the hospital calling her? They didn't deal with Malpractice cases...

"Matthew Price was brought in. You're listed as his emergency contact. Could you come to the hospital?"

Panic seized her heart. Matthew was her only friend and if something had happened to him... How would she go on without him? He'd been her rock for so long. This couldn't be happening. She'd finally managed to feel safe and content with her lot in life. Without Matt, it might fall apart all over again. She reminded herself to breathe. It'd do no good to suspect the worst before she had all the information. The hard question needed to be asked, even if she was afraid of the answer.

"Is he..."

Lana interrupted her, "He's fine—or well—as okay as he's going to be for now. The doctor can explain more when you get here."

Dani gulped. She could handle this. She dealt with more complicated problems in court. Her friend needed her and she would go to him. The case could wait. It was minor in comparison. She wasn't about to lose another friend. Leaving her best friend behind in high school had devastated her. An image of him floated through her mind, and she brushed it away. Thinking about him would only make things worse. She couldn't let her old doubts fill her now. Matt's condition was an immediate concern. The things she couldn't change had to stay firmly where they belonged...in the past.

She shook her head clear and focused on the call. "I'll be there shortly."

"Come in through the emergency room. They can direct you where to go. Mr. Price isn't in a room yet."

"Who should I ask for?" She hated to go into a situation with little to no details. The least she could do was figure out who to direct her questions to. This woman wasn't being forthcoming at all. Dani was on the brink of becoming pissed off.

"Ask to be taken to Mr. Price. When the doctor has time, he'll come by and speak with you," she replied briskly.

Dani reluctantly agreed and set the phone back down on the receiver. She stood and realized she forgot to ask who Matt's doctor was. She would have to remember to do so when she arrived at the hospital. Information was power, something she learned the hard way in law school. The more she had, the better equipped she was to handle a situation. If she was going to take care of Matt, she had to learn everything she could about his circumstances.

"Claire, hold all my calls and reschedule any appointments for either Matt or myself for next week." She paused and revised her statement, "Wait, for Matt don't reschedule at all. Cancel them and let them know we will call them back when we are able to reschedule."

She lifted her head to meet Dani's gaze. "Is everything all right?"

"I'm not sure." Dani bit her lip. A rush of anxiety filled her. "Something happened to Matt. I don't have the facts yet. When I know more, I will let you know. I'm heading to the hospital now."

Claire nodded. "I will handle the office. Please tell Matt..." She frowned and shook her head, appearing to rethink her words. "Call me when you get a handle on the situation."

Dani didn't have time to figure out what that little slip meant. Claire seemed to be even more anxious than she was. What was going on between Claire and Matt? When she had the chance she'd have to ask him. It could be her imagination.

It took her twenty achingly long minutes to get to the hospital. She ran into the emergency room after she parked her car. Tears burned at the corners of her eyes, threatening to spill freely. She fought them. They were a sign of weakness and she refused to give into them. Matt would be fine. He *would*. If she kept telling herself that she might actually believe it.

"I got a call from a..." What was that woman's name? Damn it, she forgot. The woman hadn't been helpful, and she had a name that wasn't easy to remember too. "It started with an L. Lisa... Laura..." She was usually much better with details. Dani waved her hand. "It doesn't matter. Matthew Price was brought in. I'm his emergency contact."

The nurse handling admittance in the emergency room typed away at her computer. She was probably used to frantic people in search of their loved ones. She didn't appear fazed at Dani's inability to remember the other woman's name.

She stood up and gestured. "Follow me. I will take you to Mr. Price."

Dani trailed behind her until they reached a set of double doors. The nurse lifted her identification card and held it against an electronic panel. The doors slid open to let them on the other side. Dani followed her down a few halls and into an exam room. Loud steady beeps from monitors filled the entire area. Matt lay upon the bed, still and silent.

What was visible of his body appeared to be an immense bruise of various shades of purple and blue. His eyes and the entire top of his head were covered with white gauze, and his left arm was splinted and wrapped.

"What happened?" Dani turned to the nurse. It hurt to look at him. She swallowed the lump forming in her throat and asked, "What's wrong with him?"

The nurse shook her head. Her mouth was set into a firm line. "I'm not at liberty to say. I'll let the doctor know you've arrived."

She hated not having answers. It was a simple question. The nurse should be able to tell her what happened to him. She might not be able to disclose his exact condition, but surely she knew how he came to be injured in the first place. Dani reined in her frustration. It wouldn't do any good to interrogate the nurse. The answers would be given to her as soon as the doctor came to see her. Until then, she would remain patient.

"Will Matt regain consciousness?" Dani could feel tears threatening to fall again. "He looks so…is he in pain?"

"He is sedated and has been given something for the pain. He's comfortable." The nurse shook her head again. "I can't give you any more details. I promise I'll let the doctor know you're here. He can explain it in more detail and tell you what we need from you."

Dani grabbed a chair and pulled it up to his bedside. She lifted his uninjured hand into hers and held it against her cheek. "Please have the doctor come in as soon as possible. I need to know what is wrong with my friend."

The nurse nodded and left the room.

"What's going on Matt?" She rubbed his hand with hers. She wanted to hug him tight against her and not let go. "What mess did you get yourself into?"

Matt had been her friend since the early days of college. They even went to the same law school together. After leaving her hometown of Hope Beach, and a foster family she'd been happy to forget, Matt had been a breath of life she'd not realized she needed. She'd been so lonely until she met him. He'd been her rock, the center she'd been craving to keep her balanced. Dani had grown up in a series of foster homes and never had a stable home life. Her last set of foster parents were not the loving sort, and she'd been ready to run as soon as she graduated. Only one person would have kept her in town, and he'd found someone else to build a family with.

It was her fault. She'd loved him and gave him her heart the moment she laid eyes on him. He was kind, generous, and oh so handsome. He was her first friend and the only man she would ever love. But he wasn't hers. Not anymore, and never in the way she'd dreamed of. It was her fault. If she hadn't been afraid to lose him... In the end she lost him anyway. She thought if she had him as a friend it would be enough.

Until he fell in love with someone else...

Dani hadn't factored that part in. How could she remain friends with him and get in the way of his relationship. It was clear the other woman in his life didn't like or trust her. A part of Dani didn't blame her. It had to have been obvious how much she loved Ren. If their roles had been in reverse, she'd have acted the same way. So, for him, she left. She never looked back and wished him all the happiness in the world. He was nothing but a memory now, albeit a painful one.

Matt was her present. A friend she didn't fear losing her heart to. It had been given away to someone she never planned on seeing again. Matt had a much more stable and special place in her life.

"Please be all right," she whispered. She loved Matt, but not as a woman loved a man. He was the one person she cared about, and she would move Heaven and Earth to make sure he would pull through the hell he now found himself in. Matt was all that mattered. Sometimes she wished she still had a heart to give him. Loving Matt could be so easy if she didn't still love another man.

The man who would always be in her heart, the one she'd love until the day she died. Dani believed soul mate's existed. There were different kinds for different reasons. She met the love of her life when she was a teenager. In a different time or place maybe they would have had a chance. Circumstances and her bad decisions separated them forever. She was lonely until she met Matt. He was another version of her soul mate. The true best friend she could lean on. She loved him in a different way, but never in the romantic sense.

"So the nurse tells me you're Mr. Price's emergency contact."

A voice filled the room. It was as familiar as breathing. She would have known it anywhere. It haunted her dreams and sneaked into her thoughts when she least expected it. For a brief moment she thought she might be hearing things. Had she conjured up his voice because she'd been thinking of him earlier? No, that was silly. There was no way he could actually be behind her. Dani turned slowly and blinked several times. She could feel the color draining from her cheeks. This couldn't be happening to her. "Ren?"

"Dr. Sousa, I forgot to give you Mr. Price's chart." A nurse with dark auburn hair and soft brown eyes bustled in and handed him a file.

Ren stared at Dani and didn't say a word for several seconds. He studied her in awkward silence. He was almost exactly as she remembered him. His hair was a bit shorter, and his blue eyes stole her breath. It was Ren. Having him near always had that effect on her. He turned toward the nurse, took the file out of her hand, and dismissed her with a nod. "Thank you, Lana."

Lana...that was the woman who'd called her office. Dani filed her name away for future refer- ence. She was pretty, petite, and had a no-nonsense attitude. Something Dani appreciated. The nurse nodded and left the room. Leaving Ren alone with her. He set the file down and walked over to her side. The silence in the room was palpable. She had no idea what to say to him and still wasn't completely convinced he was real. Hallucinations had never plagued her before, but there was always a first time for everything…

"Dani, I didn't realize…I should have asked Lana for a name."

Real. Definitely real. She gulped down a lump in her throat. Hell how was she supposed to deal with Ren, and Matt's situation at the same time? This was an overwhelming emotional circumstance, and she wasn't entirely sure she was up to dealing with it. She sent up a silent prayer for strength.

She shook her head. "There was no way for you to know." This was all too much. Matt was hurt and Ren was his doctor. How could life have set her on this path? Her two best friends—one's life depended on the other.

Was this the fate's way of making her face her past?

She cleared her throat and turned away from him. It hurt to look at him. He looked as amazing as she remembered. A golden-brown haired god with ocean blue eyes, pain stabbed in tiny pinpricks against her already aching heart.

"What do you need from me?"

Ren didn't answer her. Had he remained in the room with her? She didn't want to turn around and look, but he was forcing her to face him. Why did she have to deal with this? Normally she could handle anything… This was too much in one breath of time for her. The tears she'd been holding back were about to come crashing forward.

Her breath hitched as she turned to look at him. All the love she had been carrying around for him— it was still there. He was a walking reminder of what she didn't have. His gaze held such concern for her.

"Dani, perhaps we should go to my office to discuss this."

Hearing her name spoken in his voice was almost her undoing. They'd stepped into an easy pattern of familiarity, but they knew next to nothing about each other anymore. They had a past. That was it.

"Does it matter where we talk about Matt?" She looked down at her friend. "The nurse said he was sedated. I doubt he will hear any of it."

What she didn't say was she needed the buffer. She didn't know what she would say or do if she was completely alone with him. Sure Matt wasn't about to jump into the conversation, but he was better than talking about the elephant in the room. Her feelings for Ren, his lack of them for her, and the fact she'd disappeared from his life so many years ago. She hadn't even said goodbye. It would have been too difficult to face him and explain why she couldn't be in his life anymore. Jessica needed him to devote all his attention to her. Dani would have been in the way. Leaving was the only decision she could have made.

"I think you will be more comfortable there discussing his condition," he replied softly. "I have a lot to go over with you."

Ren had always been kind. This wasn't about her. Matt's condition had to be more important. It was time for her to suck it up and deal with her emotional overload. Ren wasn't going to bite her head off. It wasn't who he was.

"Fine, lead the way, Dr. Sousa."

Dani had to put up barriers and ignore her rampant emotions. He couldn't be Ren anymore. He was Matt's doctor and nothing more. Her feelings on the matter were irrelevant.

ACKNOWLEDGMENTS

This is where I thank my editor and cover artist, Victoria Miller profusely. She helps me more than I can ever say. I appreciate everything she does and that she pushes me to be better...do better. Thank you a thousand times over.

Also to Elizabeth Evans. Thank you for always being there for me and being my friend. You mean so much to me. Thanks isn't nearly enough, but it's all I have, so thank you my friend for being you.

Thanks to Aletha Boyd for taking the time to proofread. It helps a lot to have another set of eyes go over the book and find the typos that slip through. It's greatly appreciated.

ABOUT THE AUTHOR

USA TODAY Bestselling author, DAWN BROWER writes both historical and contemporary romance. There are always stories inside her head; she just never thought she could make them come to life. That creativity has finally found an outlet.

Growing up she was the only girl out of six children. She is a single mother of two teenage boys; there is never a dull moment in her life. Reading books is her favorite hobby and she loves all genres.

BB bookbub.com/authors/dawn-brower
f facebook.com/AuthorDawnBrower
twitter.com/1DawnBrower
instagram.com/1DawnBrower
g goodreads.com/dawnbrower

ALSO BY DAWN BROWER

HISTORICAL

Stand alone:

Broken Pearl

A Wallflower's Christmas Kiss

A Gypsy's Christmas Kiss

Marsden Romances

A Flawed Jewel

A Crystal Angel

A Treasured Lily

A Sanguine Gem

A Hidden Ruby

A Discarded Pearl

Marsden Descendants

Rebellious Angel

Tempting An American Princess

How to Kiss a Debutante

Loving an America Spy

Linked Across Time

Saved by My Blackguard

Searching for My Rogue

Seduction of My Rake

Surrendering to My Spy

Spellbound by My Charmer

Stolen by My Knave

Separated from My Love

Scheming with My Duke

Secluded with My Hellion

Secrets of My Beloved

Spying on My Scoundrel

Shocked by My Vixen

Smitten with My Christmas Minx

Vision of Love

Enduring Legacy

The Legacy's Origin

Charming Her Rogue

Ever Beloved

Forever My Earl

Always My Viscount

The Neverhartts

Never Defy a Vixen

Never Disregard a Wallflower

Never Dare a Hellion

Never Deceive a Bluestocking

Never Disrespect a Governess

Never Desire a Duke

CONTEMPORARY

Stand alone:

Deadly Benevolence

Snowflake Kisses

Kindred Lies

Sparkle City

Diamonds Don't Cry

Hooking a Firefly

Novak Springs

Cowgirl Fever

Dirty Proof

Unbridled Pursuit

Sensual Games

Christmas Temptation

Daring Love

Passion and Lies

Desire and Jealousy

Seduction and Betrayal

Begin Again

There You'll Be

Better as a Memory

Won't Let Go

Heart's Intent

One Heart to Give

Unveiled Hearts

Heart of the Moment

Kiss My Heart Goodbye

Heart in Waiting

Heart Lessons

A Heart Redeemed

Kismet Bay

Once Upon a Christmas

New Year Revelation

All Things Valentine

Luck At First Sight

Endless Summer Days

A Witch's Charm

All Out of Gratitude

Christmas Ever After

YOUNG ADULT FANTASY

Broken Curses

The Enchanted Princess

The Bespelled Knight

The Magical Hunt